THE BOTTLE F

For the Italian wor
to be an idyllic da
the drab monoton
There would be a
stately home; Fred
Vittorio whom sl
work bench.

It was Freda, blonde, buxom and bossy who had engineered the whole outing. She had cajoled mousey Brenda into going. She had even lent her her best purple cloak.

It was to be a triumph of a day, the culmination of all her hopes, the day when sleek, long-lashed Vittorio would claim her as his own.

Instead, it turned out to be a day of tragedy and Freda was never the same again . . .

Cambs 31-12-77

BERYL BAINBRIDGE

The Bottle Factory Outing

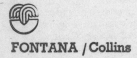

FONTANA / Collins

First published in 1974 by Gerald Duckworth & Co Ltd
First issued in Fontana Books 1975

© 1974 Beryl Bainbridge

Made and Printed in Great Britain by
William Collins Sons & Co Ltd Glasgow

for Pauline

CHAPTER ONE

The hearse stood outside the block of flats, waiting for the old lady. Freda was crying. There were some children and a dog running in and out of the line of bare black trees planted in the pavement.

'I don't know why you're crying,' said Brenda. 'You didn't know her.'

Four paid men in black, carrying the coffin on their shoulders, began to walk the length of the top landing. Below, on the first floor, a row of senior citizens in nighties and overcoats stood on their balconies ready to wave the old woman goodbye.

'I like it,' said Freda. 'It's so beautiful.'

Opulent at the windows, she leant her beige cheek against the glass and stared out mournfully at the block of flats, moored in concrete like an ocean liner. Behind the rigging of the television aerials, the white clouds blew across the sky. All hands on deck, the aged crew with lowered heads shuffled to the rails to watch the last passenger disembark.

Freda was enjoying herself. She stopped a tear with the tip of her finger and brought it to her mouth.

'I'm very moved,' she observed, as the coffin went at an acute angle down the stairs.

Brenda, who was easily embarrassed, didn't care to be seen gawping at the window. She declined to look at the roof of the hearse, crowned with flowers like a Sunday hat, as the coffin was shoved into place.

'She's going,' cried Freda, and the engine started and the black car slid away from the kerb, the gladioli and the arum lilies trembling in the breeze.

'You cry easily,' said Brenda, when they were dressing to go to the factory.

'I like funerals. All those flowers – a full life coming to a close – '

'She didn't look as if she'd had a full life,' said Brenda. 'She only had the cat. There weren't any mourners – no sons or anything.'

'Take a lesson from it then. It could happen to you. When I go I shall have my family about me – daughters – sons – my husband, grey and distinguished, dabbing a handkerchief to his lips – '

'Men always go first,' said Brenda. 'Women live longer.'

'My dear, you ought to participate more. You are too cut off from life.'

When Freda spoke like that Brenda would have run into another room, had there been one. Uneasily she said, 'I do participate. More than you think.'

'You are not flotsam washed up on the shore, without recourse to the sea,' continued Freda. She was lifting one vast leg and polishing the toe of her boot on the hem of the curtains. 'When we go on the Outing you bloody well better participate.'

'I can't promise,' said Brenda rebelliously.

Unlike Freda, whose idea it had been, the thought of the Outing filled her with alarm. It was bound to rain, seeing it was already October, and she could just imagine the dreary procession they would make, forlornly walking in single file across the grass, the men slipping and stumbling under the weight of the wine barrels, and Freda, face distorted with fury at the weather, sinking down on to the muddy ground, unwrapping her cold chicken from its silver foil, wrenching its limbs apart under the dripping branches of the trees. Of course Freda visualized it differently. She was desperately in love with Vittorio, the trainee manager, who was the nephew of Mr Paganotti, and she thought she would have a better chance of seducing him if she could get him out into the open air, away from the bottling plant and his duties in the cellar. What she planned was a visit to a Stately Home and a stroll through Elizabethan gardens, hand in hand if she had her way. The men in the factory, senses reeling at the thought of a day in the country with the English ladies, had sent their Sunday suits to the cleaners and told their wives and children that the Outing was strictly for the workers. Rossi had given Freda permission to order a mini-coach; Mr Paganotti had been persuaded to donate four barrels of wine, two white and two red.

'You should be terribly keen,' said Freda. 'All that fresh air and the green grass blowing. You should be beside yourself at the prospect.'

'Well, I'm not,' said Brenda flatly.

Freda, who longed to be flung into the midst of chaos, was astonished at her attitude. When they had first met in the butcher's shop on the Finchley Road, it had been Brenda's lack of control, her passion, that had been the attraction. Standing directly in front of Freda she had asked for a pork chop, and the butcher, reaching for his cleaver on the wooden slab, had shouted with familiarity 'Giving the old man a treat are you?' at which Brenda had begun to weep, moaning that her husband had left her, that there was no old man in her world. She had trembled in a blue faded coat with a damaged fur collar and let the tears trickle down her face. Freda led her away, leaving the offending cut of meat on the counter, and after a week they found a room together in Hope Street, and Freda learnt it wasn't the husband that had abandoned Brenda, it was she who had left him because she couldn't stand him coming home drunk every night from the Little Legion and peeing on the front step. Also, she had a Mother-in-Law who was obviously deranged, who sneaked out at dawn to lift the eggs from under the hens and drew little faces on the shells with a Biro.

It was strange it had happened to Brenda, that particular kind of experience, coming as she did from such a respectable background – private school and music lessons and summer holidays playing tennis – exchanging her semi-detached home for a remote farmhouse in Yorkshire, lying in a great brass bed with that brute of a husband, and outside the wild moors, the geese and ducks in the barn, the sheep flowing through a gap in the wall to huddle for warmth against the sides of the house. She was so unsuited for such a life, with her reddish hair worn shoulder-length and stringy, her long thin face, her short-sighted blue eyes that never looked at you properly, while she, Freda, would have been in her element – there had been white doves on the out-house roof.

It was unfair. She told her so. 'I always wanted to live in a house with a big kitchen. I wanted a mother in a string vest and a pinny who made bread and dumpling stew.'

'A string vest?' said Brenda dubiously, and Freda couldn't explain – it would have been wasted on her.

Since that first outburst in the butcher's shop, Brenda had become withdrawn and unemotional, except for her delusion that men were after her. Freda had hoped working in a factory would enrich Brenda's life. When she had seen the advertisement in the newsagent's shop she had told her it was just the sort of job they needed, even if it paid badly, seeing they could save on tube fares and lunches and wouldn't have to wear their good clothes. Brenda said she'd got no good clothes, which was the truth. Freda had given up her job as a cashier in a night club: the hours were too erratic and it meant she could never get up early enough to go for auditions. Every Thursday she bought a copy of *The Stage* and every Friday night she went to a theatrical pub and met people in the business. Nothing ever came of it. Brenda didn't do anything, apart from a little shopping. She got a postal order from her father every week, but it wasn't enough to live on.

'It's not right,' Freda told her. 'At your age you've got to think of your future.'

Brenda, who was thirty-two, was frightened at the implication: she felt she had one foot in the grave. They had gone once to a bureau on the High Street and said they were looking for temporary work in an office. They lied about their speed and things, but the woman behind the desk wasn't encouraging. Secretly Freda thought it was because Brenda looked such a fright – she had toothache that morning and her jaw was swollen. Brenda thought it was because Freda wore her purple cloak and kept flipping ash on the carpet. Freda said they needed to do something more basic, something that brought them into contact with the ordinary people, the workers.

'But a bottle factory,' protested Brenda, who did not have the same needs as her friend.

Patiently Freda explained that it wasn't a bottle factory, it was a wine factory – that they would be working alongside simple peasants who had culture and tradition behind them. Brenda hinted she didn't like foreigners – she found them difficult to get on with. Freda said it proved how puny a person she was, in mind and in body.

'You're bigoted,' she cried. 'And you don't eat enough.'

To which Brenda did not reply. She looked and kept silent, watching Freda's smooth white face and the shining feather of yellow hair that swung to the curve of her jaw. She had large blue eyes with curved lashes, a gentle rosy mouth, a nose perfectly formed. She was five foot ten in height, twenty-six years old, and she weighed sixteen stone. All her life she had cherished the hope that one day she would become part of a community, a family. She wanted to be adored and protected, she wanted to be called 'little one'.

'Maybe today,' Freda said, 'Vittorio will ask me out for a drink.' She looked at Brenda who was lying down exhausted on the big double bed. 'You look terrible. I've told you, you should take Vitamin B.'

'I don't hold with vitamins. I'm just tired.'

'It's your own fault. You should make the bloody bed properly and get a good night's kip.'

Brenda had fashioned a bolster to put down the middle of the bed and a row of books to ensure that they lay less intimately at night. Freda complained that the books were uncomfortable – but then she had never been married. At night when they prepared for bed Freda removed all her clothes and lay like a great fretful baby, majestically dimpled and curved. Brenda wore her pyjamas and her underwear and a tweed coat – that was the difference between them. Brenda said it was on account of nearly being frozen to death in Ramsbottom, but it wasn't really that. Above the bed Freda had hung a photograph of an old man sitting on a stool with a stern expression on his face. She said it was her grandfather, but it wasn't. Brenda had secretly scratched her initials on the leg of the chair nearest the window, just to prove this one was hers when the other fell apart due to Freda's impressive weight. The cooker was on the first floor, and there was a bathroom up a flight of stairs and a window on the landing bordered with little panes of stained glass. Freda thought it was beautiful. When she chose, the washing on the line, the fragments of tree and brick, were tinted pink and gold. Brenda, avoiding the coloured squares, saw only a back yard grey with soot and a stunted rambling rose that never bloomed sprawled against the crumbling surface of the wall. She felt it was unwise to see things as other than they were. For this reason she disliked the lampshade that hung in the centre of the room: when the wind blew through the gaps in the large double windows, the shade twisted in the draught, the fringing of brown silk spun round and shadows ran across the floor. She kept thinking it was mice.

'Get up,' said Freda curtly. 'I want to smooth the bed.'

It was awkward with all those books sticking up under the blankets. Freda was very houseproud, always polishing and dusting and dragging the Hoover up and down the carpet, and she made some terrible dents in in the paintwork of the skirting board. She only bothered in case Vittorio suddenly asked to accompany her home. He wasted some part of every afternoon chatting to her at her bench, all about his castle in Italy and his wealthy connections. She told him he had a chip on his shoulder, forever going on about money and position – she called him a 'Bloody Eyetie'. They had quite violent arguments and a lot of the time he spoke to her harshly, but she took it as a good sign, as love was very close to hate. She'd made Brenda promise to go straight out and walk round the streets if ever he looked like coming home with them. Only yesterday he had given her three plums in a paper bag as a present, and she'd kept the stones and put them in her jewel case in the wardrobe.

She told Brenda to carry the milk bottles downstairs. In the hall she paused and ran back upstairs to check the sheets were fairly clean, just in case.

CHAPTER TWO

Brenda broke into a run as soon as they left the house. A stream of traffic going very fast caused her to halt at the intersection of Park Road and Hope Street.

'Fool,' shouted Freda, walking leisurely behind her.

'We're late,' wailed Brenda. 'We've not been on time yet.'

'Foreigners,' Freda said carefully, 'understand about the artistic temperament.' She walked on in television serials very occasionally, either as a barmaid or a lady agitator.

'I hate being conspicuous. You know how I hate it.'

'You surprise me,' said Freda.

Brenda was so cold she was dressed onion-fashion in layers – pullovers and scarves and a double sheet of newspaper under her vest. She wore no make-up. Sometimes, when she suffered from the toothache, she affected a woollen balaclava that her husband had worn on the farm.

Freda walked towards the sweet-shop to buy her cigarettes. 'Calm yourself,' she called, as the dithering Brenda ran up and down the pavement. 'Nobody will say a word about the time. Not a bloody word.'

Brenda knew it was true. She also knew there was a reason for it, an explanation that Freda refused to credit. Freda hinted Brenda was trying to draw attention to herself.

'I ask you,' she had shouted quite loudly, 'is it likely, the way you're got up?' And she had laughed.

Brenda begged her to keep her eyes open so that she would observe the precise moment she was plucked from the bench, but Freda never bothered. She was always turned to Maria, talking about politics or the theatre, and Brenda couldn't very well tug at her arm with Rossi looking on so eagerly from behind the window of his office. Brenda disappeared for what seemed like hours, either down into the cloistered chill of the cellar or upstairs amidst the stored furniture. Freda had never noticed.

Majestically Freda came out of the sweet-shop and strolled up the street. She was like a ballroom dancer moving in time to some slow waltz, pointing her feet delicately as she advanced, swaying from side to side in her purple cloak, one hand raised slightly with wrist arched, as if she dangled a fan. She looked with interest into the basements of the Victorian houses and thought how disordered were the middle classes – the lack of carpeting, the identical shabby rocking-chairs set against the walls, the mania for stripped wood as if under the illusion they lived in log cabins in the outback. She saw herself with Vittorio, sprawled in an embrace upon the bare boards, toes pointing at the ceiling. Brenda was scurrying into the distance. as she ran she brushed the bulky side of a privet hedge with the padded shoulders of her over-large coat – the landlady had discarded it when her grand-dad died, intending it for the bin-men. Freda wouldn't walk with her dressed like that; she made her run on ahead.

The wine factory was on the corner of the street next to the Greek chip-shop. It was three storeys high with its paint-work peeling and the name PAGANOTTI on a brass plate above the door. The lorries parked in the main street and caused traffic jams. There was an alleyway and a fire escape loaded with boxes and plastic containers, and a side door made of iron, outside which Brenda was waiting, shoulders hunched against the wind.

'Please keep your eye on me. It's not much to ask.'

'Shut up,' said Freda, patting her hair into place. No matter how rushed she was for time she managed to paint the lids of her eyes cobalt blue and to coat her lashes with Vaseline.

Everyone shook hands with them when they came into

work, all the tired bottling men in their green overalls and trilby hats. One by one they took it in turn to step away from the rusted machinery slowly revolving in the centre of the floor. They left the steel rods squirting out wine, pumped up from the cellar beneath into the dark rotating bottles, bashfully to hold the cool outstretched fingers of the English ladies. Freda found the ritual charming. It established contact with the elusive Vittorio, if only fleetingly. *'Bongiorno',* she trilled, over and over.

They worked from eleven in the morning till three in the afternoon. They weren't supposed to have a break for lunch, but most days Freda bullied Brenda into going over the road to the public house to share one hot sausage and one vodka and lime. Maria, who started at eight and left at two, could not bring herself to go with them. She brought sandwiches made of salami, the left-overs from her nephew's restaurant, wrapped up in a headscarf. She wore the black dresses she had carried from Italy twenty years before, and after midday, when the damp got to her bones, she climbed into a mail bag for warmth. All the same she suffered dreadfully from chilblains, and Freda persuaded her to wear mittens. She worshipped Freda, whom she thought bold and dashing and resourceful. What style she had – the large English girl with the milk-white skin and eyelids stained the colour of cornflowers. How easily she had wrought improvements in their daily labour. Refusing to stoop over the wooden labelling bench, she had complained loudly of a pain in her splendid back and found beer crates for them to sit on. She had purchased rubber gloves from the Co-op to protect her mauve and shining nails; she had insisted that the Mrs Brenda do the same. She had contrived an Outing into the landscape, a day under the sky and the trees. Best of all, she had condoned the wearing of mail bags and advised the use of mittens. At the sight of Freda, Maria's large pale face flushed pink with pleasure; she stamped her feet to ease her chilblains and swung her head from side to side. But for the cramp in her knee, she would have risen and genuflected.

'Hey up,' said Freda, when the round of hand-shaking

was completed. 'You're wearing your sexy nylons again.' She was looking at the grey football socks on Maria's stumpy legs.

With joy Maria rocked back and forth on her beer crate. 'Aye, aye,' she moaned, rolling her eyes and darting glances at Freda, magnificent in her purple trousers and hand-made Cossack boots. She understood little of the conversation: the English girl gabbled her words so fast.

The ground floor of the factory was open to the street and the loading bay. In summer the stone walls kept the bottling area cool, in winter the temperature dropped below freezing. The men stamped their feet, blew on their fingers and pulled their trilby hats about their ears. On the stone columns that supported the floor above, the men had glued pictures from magazines – a view of Naples, a stout young lady standing in a garden, someone's son who had studied hard at night, bettered himself and passed an examination. Above the cardboard boxes stacked in rows twelve foot high, there was a picture of the Virgin holding her baby and a plaque of the Sacred Heart, sore wounded, nailed like a football rosette to the green painted wall. The work-benches faced a row of windows overlooking the back wall of the chip-shop and an inch of sky.

In vain Freda had tried to tell the men how low their wages were by other standards, how severely they were exploited. They listened politely but without comprehension. To them Mr Paganotti was a wise father, a *padrone* who had plucked them from the arid slopes of their mountain region and set them down in a land of milk and honey. What did she know of their lives before the coming of Mr Paganotti? They were *contadini* who had grown wheat and corn and grapes, but only with tremendous labour, such as made their work in the factory seem like one long afternoon of play. Sometimes they had managed a harvest of plums and apples. They had kept chickens and a cow or two. In every way they were peasants, dulled by poverty. But then there had been a miracle. Mr Paganotti in his infinite wisdom had picked four men from the village of Caprara and brought them to Hope Street, and when they had settled they sent for their wives and their sons and their cousins and they saved their wages and together bought one house, then two, until in time each owned a little brick house in the suburbs with hot water running from a tap and a lavatory that flushed. Gone were the terracotta roofs of the farmhouses they had known, the stone sinks, the primitive wood-burning stoves. Only the religious pictures remained and the statues of Christ on the cross. As the children of the first generation of workers grew up, their parents were diligent in conveying just how munificent was the generosity of Mr Paganotti. They remained a close and isolated community. No one ever left the factory to take other employment; the sons were encouraged to go on to University and become doctors and accountants. Those who did not have the ability joined their fathers on the factory floor. They had changed little in thirty years – even Mr Paganotti could not understand the language they spoke, the *dialetto bolognese* that was older than Italian and closer to French. If there was a confrontation between himself and one of the cellar-men, Rossi the manager, who alone had adapted himself to the English way of life, was called in to act as interpreter. In spite of their good fortune they still stood like beasts of the field, tending Mr Paganotti's machines.

It was Brenda's job to rinse out the sponges in the morning and to tip the glue from the pot into the shallow trays on the benches. She didn't mind fetching the glue pot from beneath old Luigi's place, but she had to go to the Ladies' washroom to wet the sponges. She always ran straight across the factory floor without looking to right or left, in case Rossi caught sight of her, flying through the door of the washroom and out again with her sponges dripping, as if she was the last runner in a relay race. It looked as if she was really zealous and interested in what she was doing.

'You overdo it,' said Freda. She had slapped the little glittering labels into the glue and stacked a dozen bottles of wine in a neat triangle on the bench top. She maintained it was all the same wine – it was just the labels that were different. Today it was Rose Anjou and it was fractionally pinker than the Beaujolais – it could have been the tint of the glass bottles or dilution with water.

Brenda had only used one tray of labels when she was distracted by old Luigi at the far end of the line of benches. He stood with his feet wide apart to balance himself, on lengths of planking laid over the concrete floor to lessen the cold. He was muttering and pulling faces at the women. Freda, as she worked, talked incessantly and dramatically. She twisted and turned on her beer crate, she thumped the bottles down into the cardboard box at her side, she stamped her feet for emphasis. Each time that she got up to reach with her rubber-gloved fingers for another label, and sank backwards on to her upturned crate, the frail old man rose in the air and settled again. As the morning wore on and he trotted more and more frequently to refill his little plastic beaker at the wine barrel reserved for the men, so his muttering became wilder, his glances less discreet. He loathed the English women; he held them in scorn. He would not shake hands with them in the morning; he refused to contribute to the Outing. Alone of all the Italians in the factory, he neither admired nor took pleasure in the appearance of Freda; if he could, he would have burnt her beer crate in the market square.

Freda was saying to Maria: 'You must support the Unions. It's your duty. It's no good burying your head in the sand. Know what I mean?'

'Aye, aye,' intoned Maria, wiping gently the neck of the bottle with her honey-coloured sponge.

'We could do with a bloody Union man here – the cold, the conditions. Talk about A Day in the Life Of – don't you know about the Factories Act?'

Above the hostile shoulder of Luigi, Brenda saw Rossi's face at the window of the office. She tried to avert her eyes, but he was jumping up and down, jerking his curly head in the direction of the door and smiling with all his teeth showing.

'Freda,' she hissed, out of the corner of her mouth.

'We shouldn't be working in a temperature like this,' said Freda. 'It's against the law.'

'Freda — he's at it again.'

'Old Piggynotty could be prosecuted.' Down slammed Freda's boots on the planking. The smell of talcum powder, dry and sweet, rose from the armpits of her grey angora jumper as she jabbed with her sponge at a completed bottle of Rose Anjou. 'Know what I mean?'

As if lassoed by an invisible rope, Brenda was dragged from her place at the bench. Unwillingly she passed the grimacing Luigi and walked between the avenue of shelves filled with brandy bottles, towards the office. Rossi stood in the doorway waiting for her. 'I have something to show you,' he confided in a feverish manner, and was off, trotting towards the pass door, peering over his plump shoulder at her to make certain she was following. She was convinced all the men were looking at her. They tittered and insinuated, anchored to the bottling plant shuddering in the centre of the floor. They knew, she was sure, about Rossi: his childless marriage to an elderly wife called Bruna, his frequent trips into the basement, his sudden disappearance into the groaning lift in the corner behind the boxes, and always, like the smoke from a cigarette, herself trailing in his wake. Looking very serious, as if the matter was both urgent and highly secret, she descended the steps into the cellar.

Rossi was running across the stone floor beneath the white-washed arches hung with cobwebs. He made a small dandified skip into the air as he leapt the rubber hose that lolled like a snake between the barrels of wine. Reverently she tiptoed deeper into the shadows cast by the little hanging lights. But for the sour smell of vinegar and the constant hum of machinery as the hose pumped wine to the floor above, she might have been in church. Rossi was bobbing about in the darkness, whispering 'Missy Brenda, come over here. I have a little drink for you.' He had a white overall, to show he was more important than the men, with PAGANOTTI embroidered on the pocket, and he wore suede shoes stained with wine.

'How kind of you,' said Brenda.

He took a medicine bottle from his pocket and poured the contents into two glasses that he kept on a shelf in one of the alcoves, ready for when he lured her down there. She had only been working in the factory for four weeks and it had started on her third day. He'd said then she ought to learn more about the cooling process.

'You like?'

'Yes, thank you very much.'

'You like me?'

'Oh yes, you're very nice.'

He was holding her wrist, tipping the glass backwards, trying to make her drink more rapidly. It was a kind of liqueur brandy, very hot and thick like Syrup of Figs, and it always made her feel silly. She could feel him trembling.

'What's it called?' she asked him, though she knew.

'Marsala. You are a nice girl – very nice.'

She couldn't think how to discourage him – she didn't want to lose her job and she hated giving offence. He had a funny way of pinching her all over, as if she was a mattress whose stuffing needed distributing more evenly. She stood there wriggling, saying breathlessly 'Please don't, Rossi,' but he tickled and she gave little smothered laughs and gasps that he took for encouragement.

'You are a nice clean girl.'

'Oh, thank you.'

He was interfering with her clothes, pushing his hands beneath her tweed coat and plucking away at her jumpers and vest, shredding little pieces of newspaper with his nails. She tried to have a chat with him to calm him down.

'I'm so excited about the election, Rossi.'

'So many clothes.'

'Please don't. Are *you*? Oh stop it.'

'Freda says she's going to vote Communist.'

'Why you have so much clothes?'

'You like me?' he pleaded, pinching the skin of her back as much as he was able.

'Don't do that. Consider –'

'Why don't you like me?'

'Your wife. I do like you, I do really. We saw a funeral today. It was a nice funeral.'

He didn't know what she meant. He was trying to kiss her. He had a mouth like a baby's, sulky, with the underlip drooping, set in a round dimpled face. Suck, suck, suck, went his moist lips at her neck.

'There were lots of flowers. Freda cried when she saw the coffin.'

He paused, startled. In the gloom his eyebrows rose in bewilderment. 'A funeral? Your mammy has died?' Shocked, he left off trying to unravel her defences of wool and tweed and paper. She didn't know what to say. She was very tempted to assent.

'Well, in a manner of speaking – more Freda's than mine.'

'Freda's mammy is dead?'

She hung her head as if overcome, thinking of Al Jolson down on one knee with one hand in its white glove, upraised. Her own hand, unnaturally pink in its rubber covering, hovered above his shoulder. She was still clutching her sponge.

In the Ladies' washroom Freda was mystified. She combed her hair at the blotched mirror and asked suspiciously: 'What have we got the day off for? Why have I got to take you home?'

Brenda didn't reply. She was adjusting her clothing, shaking free the fragments of paper that fell from her vest.

'Have you got your toothache again?' Freda was annoyed at having to leave early. It didn't suit her; she hadn't had her talk with Vittorio. 'Look at the state of you. You've got cobwebs in your hair.'

'I'm taking you home,' said Brenda. 'On account of your mammy.'

'Me what?'

'I had to say she wasn't well.' She looked at Freda, who for once was speechless. Her mother had died when she was twelve and she had been brought up by an aunt in Newcastle.

'Actually I said we went to her funeral. I couldn't help it, Freda. You never take any notice of me.'

She was whispering in case Rossi was outside the door listening. Freda started to laugh – she never did anything quietly.

'Sssh,' said Brenda desperately, jumping up and down in embarrassment, releasing a fresh fall of newsprint on to the washroom floor.

In the alleyway, Patrick, the Irish van driver, was inhaling a cigarette. Elbow at an angle and shoulders hunched, he stared at them curiously through a cloud of smoke.

'She's hysterical,' explained Brenda, gripping the giggling Freda fiercely by the arm and steering her out into the street.

Later, in the security of the sparsely furnished room, Freda was inclined to get at the truth. 'In the cellar?' she queried. 'But what does he do?'

'Nothing really. He sort of fumbles.'

'Fumbles?' repeated Freda and snorted to suppress laughter. 'Does he feel your chests?'

'All over, really,' admitted Brenda, not liking to go into details – Freda could be very crude in her humour if given the facts. 'Sometimes we go upstairs among all that old furniture.'

'Upstairs? When?'

'Often. I told you, but you wouldn't listen.'

Freda couldn't get over it. She stared at Brenda lying full length upon the bed like a neglected doll – cobwebs stuck in her hair, her mouth slightly open and two little pegs of teeth protruding.

'I don't understand you at all. You must be mad. You're not telling me he rushes out while we're all bottling away and ties you up with his bootlaces and rushes off into the cellar? You're not telling me I wouldn't have noticed something?'

Brenda had no reply to that.

'You shouldn't have talked to him so much. You're always talking to him, mouthing away at him as if he's stone deaf.'

Brenda gazed up at the ceiling defensively, the padded shoulders of her coat grotesquely lifted about her ears.

'I'm only saying my words clearly. His English is poor.'

'You look like Edward G. Robinson lying there.'

'You talk to Vittorio,' cried Brenda, stung by Freda's unkindness. She wanted sympathy and understanding, not criticism.

'That's different,' Freda said, and was forlornly aware it was the truth. Vittorio wasn't rushing her down into the cellar to fumble at her chests. She knew Brenda wasn't making it up. Though she lacked imagination, Brenda would go to any lengths rather than cause herself embarrassment. It was her upbringing. As a child she had been taught it was rude to say no, unless she didn't mean it. If she was offered another piece of cake and she wanted it she was obliged to refuse out of politeness. And if she didn't want it she had to say yes, even if it choked her. It was involved but understandable. There had been other small incidents that illustrated her extraordinary capacity for remaining passive while put upon. There had been the man on the bus who felt her leg almost to her knickers without her saying anything, until she had to move because it was her stop and then she'd said, 'Excuse me, I'm sorry.' And the woman with the trumpet who had stopped her in the street and asked her if she could borrow a room to practise in. Brenda loathed music. When Freda opened the door to the trumpet player and told her what to do with her trumpet, Brenda hid behind the wardrobe.

'Why didn't you tell me sooner?' asked Freda more gently – she looked so dusty and pathetic lying there – 'I would have put him in his place.'

'I did,' protested Brenda, 'often.'

Freda started to laugh again. 'How on earth did you say my mother had died.'

'I didn't,' said Brenda. 'He did. I was trying to stop him fiddling with me and I mentioned the funeral we saw this morning.'

'You driva me wilda,' mimicked Freda. 'Justa when I thinka I have you in my graspa you talka abouta da funerelo —'

'Stop it,' Brenda said.

'You putta me offa ma spaghetti—' And Freda shook with laughter.

Sulkily Brenda closed her eyes.

After a moment Freda remembered Vittorio and decided she would go downstairs and ring up Maria to ask her to pop in for a cup of tea. If Rossi had told everyone about her loss it was quite possible Vittorio felt sad for her. Perhaps he had said something tender when he heard the news — like 'Poor child — poor grieving child' — maybe he was only waiting for an excuse to come round and offer his condolences. She had to know.

'Does Rossi ever get his thingy out?' she asked, looking in her purse for money.

Brenda pretended to be asleep; she stirred on the bed and sighed as if she were dreaming. It took some time to bring Maria to the telephone. Such a thing had never happened to her before at work and Freda was worried the pips would go before her message was understood. She had to bellow down the phone to explain who she was. Brenda could hear her quite plainly.

'Maria, Maria. It's me, Freda. You know — Freda — Maria —' She sounded as if she was going to burst into the love song from *West Side Story*. 'Maria . . . I want you to come to tea . . . this afternoon . . . after work . . . Can you hear me, Maria? . . . to tea. Here at my house. You come here. No, today . . . to Freda. No I don't want any tea . . . I want to give you some . . .'

'Is she coming?' asked Brenda.

'God knows,' said Freda, and she went upstairs to the bathroom, taking a pan of water with her to flush down the lavatory. The cistern had been broken for ten days and the landlady said she couldn't find a plumber to mend it. Only Freda was inconvenienced. Brenda, who would have died rather than let the other occupants of the house know she used the toilet, usually went round the corner to the tube station.

Maria came at half-past two carrying a packet of tea and a bag of sugar. She entered the room timidly, her hands in their darned mittens, outstretched.

'La povera orfanella,' she murmured with emotion, embracing Freda, burying her head in the girl's ample shoulder. Awkwardly she patted her back and made little mewing sounds, and when she emerged again her face held such an expression of genuine perplexity and pain that it awakened feelings of remorse in Brenda.

Brenda sat Maria in the armchair by the hearth, to warm herself at the gas fire. Freda moved about the room slowly and with dignity, emptying tea-leaves into the china pot, putting the blue cups on the table, ready for the kettle to boil. Now and then she would stare out of the window with a far-away look in her eyes, as if she was remembering lost faces and lost laughter and the joy of a mother's love. After a decent interval, when the tea was poured and the biscuit tin handed round, she asked:

'And what did Vittorio say? Did he say anything?'

'Pah,' exclaimed Maria contemptuously, slapping the air with the flat of her hand. 'What could he say? Nobody work the day of their Mammy's funeral.'

'I mean, was he sorry?'

When she understood, Maria said Vittorio had looked very sad. They were all sad, but not so sad as Mr Rossi; he was the saddest of them all, pale and dejected-looking as if it was a personal loss.

'She's in love with Vittorio,' Brenda said quickly, in case Freda flew into a paddy on the spot and explained the exact reason for Mr Rossi's dejection. Maria, after an initial moment of surprise, her mouth open, her eyes bewildered, stamped her feet approvingly on the threadbare carpet. Such a match – the tall young landowner and the blonde English girl built like a tree. She recalled she could read the future in the tea-cups; a cook had taught her when she was in service in a house in Holland Park. She sat well forward in the armchair, black-clad knees wide apart, and stared into the depths of Freda's cup.

'There is a tall man,' she began, 'and a journey.'

Brenda withdrew into a corner of the room, seating herself at the table beside the window. Across the road on the balcony of the third floor an elderly woman in a blue dressing-gown and a hat with a rose pinned to the brim waved and gesticulated for help. Brenda knew her gas fire had blown up or she was out of paraffin or the cat had gone missing. It was unfortunate that Freda had rented a room opposite a building devoted to the old and infirm – there was always someone in need of assistance. Once Freda had become involved with a Miss Deansgate on the second floor, who had been a milliner for royalty; and every day for three weeks she took her bowls of soup and cups of tea, feeding her drop by drop from a tin spoon with a long handle that Miss Deansgate claimed had belonged to Queen Victoria's butler. Freda took Brenda to visit her, but she didn't enjoy it – the old woman had no stockings and her ankles were dirty and she sat on the lavatory and had to be helped back to bed. There was a funny smell in the living-room. The sheets were yellow and the frill of the pillow-case stained, as if she dribbled as she slept. Miss Deansgate begged Freda not to let the ambulance take her away; but she was dying, and in the end they laid her on the stretcher under a red blanket, looking very cheerful and Christmassy, and off she went, sliding a little on her canvas bed, as they bore her at a slant down the flight of stairs. She didn't come back, and Freda used the butler's spoon with the long handle to eat her porridge with in the morning.

Resolutely Brenda turned her eyes away from the woman with the rose in her hat. She looked at Freda and Maria by the fire, crouched over the drained cup as if the future lay there like a photograph. The murmurings of their voices and the hiss of the gas fire merged. A memory came to her. She was walking down a lane between green fields, bending her head to watch her own two feet in shiny shoes pacing the grey road. Behind her someone urged her to hurry; she could feel in the small of her back the round insistent tip of an umbrella propelling her forwards. She stumbled on the rough road, and as she fell she saw out of the corner of her eye a single scarlet poppy blowing in the brown ditch. She opened her eyes quickly, thinking 'Why can't they leave me alone?' and she was still there on the balcony, the woman demanding attention. Brenda wanted to bang on the window and tell her to go away. She hated the implied need, the intrusion on her privacy. Life was absurd, she thought, bouncing her up and down as if she were a rubber ball. She longed to lose height and roll away into a corner and be forgotten. Distress at her own conciliatory nature rose in her throat and lodged there like a stone. She swallowed and pouted her lips.

Freda found the fortune-telling satisfactory, though the reference to men in uniform and horses galloping was difficult to understand. She had a cousin in the navy but she knew nothing about horses. There was a lot of weeping and wailing and people walking in procession – that was the funeral of course. She was going on a long journey by land and sea – it could only refer to the Outing; possibly there would be a lake in the grounds of the Stately Home and she and Vittorio would drift beneath the branches of a weeping willow, alone in a rowing boat. She would trail her hand in the water and tilt her head so that any sunlight available would catch her golden hair and blind him as he rowed. She wasn't sure about the white dress Maria saw, a long flowing dress with flowers at the waist. White was not her colour – she preferred something more definite. Maria visualized problems, seeing Freda wasn't a Catholic, and Freda said actually she was very high-church and often went to mass. She was a little taken aback at what Maria implied – she herself had not been thinking along such ambitious lines.

'I'm not keen on white, am I?' she asked, looking over her shoulder for confirmation, and saw Brenda at the table, her head silhouetted against the panes of glass, the room grown dark and the sky lying yellow above the roof tops, as if snow was on the way. 'It can't snow,' she cried, striding to the window and peering out into the street. 'Not with the Outing next week.'

She shook Brenda by the shoulder as if asking for a denial and saw she had been weeping.

In bed that night Freda wanted to know what had been wrong.

'You were crying. Were you upset about Rossi?'

'I wasn't crying. It was your cigarette smoke.'

'Shall I give Rossi a piece of my mind? I could say I was going to inform Mr Paganotti.' She was elated at the prospect. She saw herself confronting the foreign capitalist at his desk. While she was about it she would tell him the conditions in his factory were sub-standard.

'Don't you dare,' said Brenda. 'I don't want any fuss.'

Below in the street she heard the distant tipsy singing of Irishmen leaving the public house on the corner. From the embankment came the low demented wail of the express as it left London for the North.

'Don't you miss the country?' Freda asked. 'The long quiet nights?'

'It wasn't quiet,' said Brenda, thinking of the cries of sheep, the snapping of twigs in the hedge as cattle blundered in the dark field, the tiny scratchings of shrews on the oilcloth of the kitchen shelf. 'Once his mother locked me in the barn with the geese.'

'Whatever for?'

'She just did. She shouted things outside and threw stones at the tin roof. The geese didn't like it.'

'What things?'

'This and that.'

'What did he say when you told him?'

'I didn't. I didn't like.'

'You know,' cried Freda, sitting up in bed and dislodging the faded pink eiderdown, 'you're a born victim, that's what you are. You ask for trouble. One day you'll go too far.' She lay down again and rubbed her toes together to warm them. 'It's probably all that crouching you did under dining-room tables during the war.'

'I never. I was never a war baby.' Brenda wished she would stop getting at her. Freda had a way of talking late at night that unwound her and sent her off into sleep while Brenda was left wide awake and anxious.

'It did make sense,' said Freda. 'The tall man and the journey.'

'That dress—' Brenda said.

'I don't get that. I'm not keen on white.'

'It's a wedding dress,' said Brenda.

All night Freda heaved and flounced beyond the line of books and the bolster encased in red satin. She flung her arm across the pillow and trapped strands of Brenda's hair. From her throat, as she dreamed, came the gurgle of unintelligible words. Brenda huddled on the extreme edge of the bed, holding her share of the blankets in both fists, staring at the cream-painted door shimmering in the light of the street lamp. She remembered her husband coming home from the Legion, dragging her from her bed to look at the moon through a telescope. She hated treading through the wet grass with the hem of her nightgown clinging to her ankles and him belching from his intake of Newcastle brown ale. He balanced the telescope on the stone wall and held it steady while she squatted shivering, leap-frog fashion, amidst the nettles, and squinted up at the heavens. The size of the moon, magnified and close, appalled her; she shrank from its size and its stillness, as it hung there like some great golf ball struck into the clouds. She shut her eyes at the memory, and unbidden came a picture of the grey farmhouse she had left, the glimmer of birch trees down by the stream, the vast curve of the worn and ancient moors rolling beyond the yard. It had been spring when she had gone there as a bride; there were lambs lying limp in the field, and he had freshly painted the windowsills for her and the rain barrel and the five-barred gate leading on to the moor. Her wedding dress, chosen and paid for by her mother, had been of cream lace with a little cloth hat to match, sewn with lilies of the valley. She wanted to wear a string of simple daisies about her neck, but Mother said she didn't have to look like a fool even if she was one. At the reception, when she stood with her new husband, Stanley, to greet their guests, his mother had leaned forward to kiss her on the cheek and bitten her ear.

She dozed and woke as Freda turned violently, tumbling books over the curve of the diving bolster. It happened every night, the pitching of books into Brenda's half of the bed, and she lay with them digging into her shoulder and her hip, making no effort to dislodge them, her hands thrust into the pockets of her overcoat for warmth. At five the bed quivered as the tube began to rumble beneath the waking street. Across the park the gibbons in the zoo leapt to the top of their wire cages and began to scream.

CHAPTER THREE

Brenda picked up two bottles of brandy and made small sounds of disapproval. 'Dear me,' she said, 'these are awful mucky.'

Save for old Luigi working away like a conveyor belt, she was alone. Rossi had gone into the city with Mr Paganotti, the men were herded into the concrete bunker at the rear of the building and Maria was eating her salami sandwiches on a heap of sacks near the loading bay. Tut-tutting as she went, Brenda grasped the bottles in her arms and walked to the washroom. Freda's shopping basket on wheels, loaded with dirty washing, stood against the wall. She put the bottles on the stone floor and began to drag Mr Paganotti's wardrobe away from the door of the first toilet. Having made a space big enough for her to squeeze through, she snatched one bottle of brandy by the neck, placed her back to the door and shoved. It was jammed. Turning round in the confined space, she leant against the wardrobe and kicked out violently with her shoe. The door sprang open and thudded against the wall. She put the brandy behind the lavatory bowl, closed the door and dragged the wardrobe back into place. Trembling, she carried the remaining bottle to the sink and dabbed at it with her sponge. 'Never again, God,' she murmured. 'Never again.'

Freda had planned it. She said she'd better stay at home for a few days seeing she was in mourning. They would think it callous otherwise, now that they knew of her loss. She bet anything old Piggynotty wouldn't pay her for time off. It was sensible to take a sample of the firm's products in lieu of wages.

'I can't do it,' Brenda said desperately. 'I'll have a heart attack.'

'You'll have one if you don't,' warned Freda menacingly. What with the cost of living and the oil crisis they deserved something to make life more bearable. 'Look at us,' she said brutally, 'the way we scrape along. Never a penny over at the end of the week. We can't afford to breathe.'

'We never could,' said Brenda. 'It's never been any different.'

She bent down and adjusted a vest that had draped itself over the side of the shopping basket. It was perfectly clean. Freda had just thrown anything in, mainly clothing from Brenda's drawer. The door opened behind her and the bog-roll man entered the washroom, his arms full of newspapers. He wasn't supposed to go near the toilets until after four o'clock, when all the women had gone home. He was short and bulky with a little moustache thin as a pencil line along his lip.

'I have come to place the toilet rolls,' he said, looking at her in a bold way and lingering on the bolstered front of her tweed coat. 'There are no rolls,' he continued. 'I have a shortage.'

'This was awfully dirty,' said Brenda, giving a last wipe with her sponge at the glistening bottle of brandy, and moving to the door. He put both arms out to capture her, hugging her to his green overalls. He smelt of wine and garlic and Jeyes' fluid.

'You want to give me a little kiss?'

'No, not really,' she said, smiling politely and shaking her head so that the bristles on his chin scraped her cheek.

Tearing herself free she stumbled from the washroom and ran back to her beer crate and her labels. She supposed it was the fumes from the wine that kept them all in a constant state of lust. It wasn't as if she set out to be desirable.

Maria appeared from the direction of the loading bay, a beaker in her hand, walking very fast and taking tiny steps as if she was still in her mail bag.

'You're early,' said Brenda. 'You've another ten minutes till the hooter goes.'

'I am to look in the box,' Maria told her, waving her arm in the air and spilling Beaujolais on to the floor. 'I am wanting shoes.'

In the corner, beneath the burglar alarm, were two large crates filled with old clothing of all descriptions. Mr Paganotti had a large number of elderly relatives living and dying in England, and hardly a month went by without his becoming the chief beneficiary of yet another will. A few choice articles of furniture he kept for his mansion near Windsor. Some things he sent to the salerooms; others he stored in the washroom, or upstairs on the first floor. The rest, the debris of a lifetime, he placed in boxes on the factory floor for the benefit of his workers. There were numerous pyjamas and nightgowns, golfing shoes in two tones, yellow stays and white-flannel trousers and striped waistcoats mouldy with damp. There was a notice pinned to the wall, stating in Italian that Mr Paganotti was delighted if his employees found use for the contents – 'Please put 2p in the tea-caddy placed for the purpose.' Rossi emptied the caddy every two days in case Patrick the van driver was tempted to help himself to the proceeds.

Brenda was thirsty. She tried sipping Maria's wine, but it gave her an ache at the back of her jaw.

'Oooh,' she wailed, 'it's horrible.'

Maria, still rummaging for shoes, cackled with laughter

and threw ties, and undergarments of incredible dimensions, on to the floor.

The machine Mr Paganotti had provided for hot drinks was out of order. When Brenda inserted her metal token and pressed the button marked 'Cocoa,' a thin stream of soup trickled into her cup. Patrick, come in from the street to be out of the wind, smiled at her sympathetically. He never knew what to do with himself in the lunch hour – the men he worked with couldn't understand a word he uttered, and Rossi treated him with suspicion, seeing he was Irish, following him about the factory in case he slipped a bomb beneath the cardboard boxes and blew them all to pieces.

'Look at that,' said Brenda. 'It's never cocoa.'

'The machine's busted,' he told her, giving it an enormous clout with his fist. He had large hands, discoloured with brown freckles, and badly bitten nails. One ear was slightly swollen where he had banged it falling down the steps of the Princess Beatrice the previous night, and there was a cut on his lip.

'Everything breaks,' said Brenda. 'All sorts of things break down these days. Electric kettles and washing machines and telephones.'

'You're right at that,' he agreed, jingling the coins in the pocket of his overalls and nodding his cropped head. He would have suited long hair, Brenda thought. It would have toned down his ears and covered his neck, which was broad and mottled with old adolescent scars.

'Our toilet's been broken for three weeks,' she told him. 'We can't get a plumber. The landlady's tried.'

'Is that a fact? Broken is it?'

'Plumbers don't live here any more,' explained Brenda, echoing what Freda had told her. 'It's on account of the high rents. Plumbers can't afford to live. It's the same with window cleaners,' she added.

'I'll fix it for you,' he said. And too late she realized what she had done.

'Oh no really, there's no need,' she protested.

But he wouldn't be put off. 'I'll be glad to. I'm good at the plumbing. Will I bring the tools round after work?'

'It's not my toilet,' said Brenda. 'I'm not sure that the land-lady – '

'I'll fetch the wherewithal from me lodgings and be round when I'm finished.'

'You're very kind,' said Brenda feebly, and returned with her beaker of soup to the bench. She stared at a bottle of Château Neuf du Pape and dreaded what Freda would say. She could almost hear her – 'You did what? You asked that lout from the bogs of Tipperary to mend our loo?' She wondered if she could sneak him upstairs without Freda knowing, or the landlady for that matter. Perhaps she could persuade him to wrap a duster round the end of his hammer.

Freda was not enjoying being off work. She hadn't the money to go down town and enjoy her leisure. She polished the surrounds of the floor and wedged the window open with Brenda's tennis racket. The room lacked character, she thought, looking critically at the yellow utility furniture and the ladies in crinolines walking in pairs across the wallpaper. There was no colour scheme – nothing matched; there was no unity of design. Every time she made some little improve-ment, like arranging a curtain round the washbasin near the door, it only drew attention to the cracked tiles and the yards of antiquated piping climbing in convoluted loops up the wall. On the shelf she had improvised above the fireplace were some paperbacks, two library books and a bottle of H.P sauce that Brenda had carelessly placed. Dissatisfied by al she saw, she went discontentedly on to the landing and carried the milk bottles downstairs. Lying on the doormat was an envelope addressed to her. When she opened it she thought she might faint. It was as if life until this moment had been spent underground or beneath the sluggish water of a river. Now, as she read the words he had written, she shot to the surface, up into the blinding sunlight and the sweet-tasting air:

My dear Freda,

   If it is permissible may I call after work to offer my respects.

                                    Your friend,
                                    Vittorio.

She clutched the note to her throat and flew in her fluffy bedroom-slippers up the stairs. Why can't life always be like this, she thought, smiling and smiling at the lovely room with its cheerful wallpaper and the gay curtain that hid the waste-pipe of the washbasin. She revolved slowly in front of the open window, the street turning with her: the shining bonnets of the cars at the kerb, the spearheads of the painted railings, the thin black trees that were bouncing in the wind. Above the gardens devoid of leaf save for laurel bush and privet hedge, the pigeons rose and dipped and rose again, lifting to the rooftops. A woman in a long plaid skirt blew like a paper boat along the pavement.

   Freda couldn't stop smiling. She closed the window and boiled a kettle of water, reaching to the shelf above the cooker for her toilet bag with her own special soap and her own clean flannel. She'd had to hide her things from Brenda, who was less than fussy – who could wipe her neck or her shoes on the dishcloth or her underclothes, all with equal impartiality, if nothing else was available. She'd have to tell her to go out for the evening. Anywhere would do: there was a new film on at the Odeon called *Super Dick*. She carried the blue plastic bowl filled with warm water into the living-room and knelt in front of the gas fire. Grown solemn now and a little peaked, the tender sensual smile gone from her mouth, she curled her pudgy toes on the worn hearth rug and began to wash herself. It would be nice to buy a piece of steak for Vittorio. She couldn't afford any for herself, but he'd appreciate her appetite was poor the day after her mother's funeral. And she'd provide a salad of lettuce and green peppers and make a real dressing of garlic and lemon juice, such as he was used to. As for Brenda, she could go to the chippie for her supper. She was always saying she didn't care for food, that it was sheer affectation to put herbs in things. People who baked food in the oven, she said, were daft – you could fry everything in a pan twice as quick. Despite her private schooling and her advantages, she'd been brought up on Spam and chips and powdered eggs, and it was no wonder her husband Stanley had gone to the Little Legion every night. She couldn't understand why suddenly she felt such resentment towards Brenda – the thought of her was spoiling her anticipation of the night to come. She frowned and slapped the soapy flannel against the soft contours of her arm. It's my room, she told herself. I found it. I have every right to take my chances, to live my life. She felt refined out of existence by the sameness and regularity of each day, the brushing of her clothes in the morning and the cleaning of her teeth at night. 'There is something more,' she murmured, her lips moving, her eyes fixed on the mutilated pattern of the rug. 'I am not Brenda – I do want something.' She had been squeezing the flannel in her hands, and the carpet was quite sodden with water. Shuffling backwards on her knees she dried herself on a towel. It would have been better if Vittorio had given her more time to prepare for his visit: she hated rushing down town and returning home with minutes to spare, her face all red from the hair-dryer. How should she behave when he came? There was no question of outright seduction – not when she was so recently bereaved. Perhaps she could be silent and rather wistful – not exactly droopy, but less aggressive than he had previously known her – so as to arouse his protective feelings. Come the day of the Outing she might then lay her hand on his sleeve and thank him for his understanding. Absently she stroked the edge of the wooden fender, thick with dust, and tilted her head backwards to avoid the heat of the fire which already had begun to mottle the smoothness of her pale cheeks. She stared at the ceiling and her mouth opened to emit a sound half-way between a sigh and a groan – 'Aaah,' she went, kneeling as if in supplication. 'Aaaah, Vittorio!' Was she right about hi feelings for her? He must like her. Otherwise why did he spend every afternoon chatting to her? And she'd seen the way his eyes flickered up and down her jumper when he thought she wasn't watching. He did fancy her, but how could she encourage him? God knows what Brenda had said or done to get Rossi into such a state of randy expectancy, but whatever it was it wouldn't work for Vittorio. He was a man of sensibilities and everything was against her— his background, his nationality, the particular regard he had for women or a category of womanhood to which she did not belong. By the strength of her sloping shoulders, the broad curve of her throat, the dimpled vastness of her columnar thighs, she would manœuvre him into her arms. I will be one of those women, she thought, painted naked on ceilings, lolling amidst rose-coloured clouds. She straightened and stared at a chair. She imagined how she might mesmerize him with her wide blue eyes. Wearing a see-through dressing-gown chosen from a Littlewoods' catalogue, she would open the door to him: 'Forgive me, I have been resting—the strain you know. My mother was particularly dear to me—' All Italians, all foreigners were dotty about their mothers; he would expect it of her. She would not actually have to gnash her teeth but imply that she did so— internally. Rumpling her newly washed hair, the black nylon sleeve of her gown sliding back to reveal one elbow, she would press her hand to her brow and tell him the doctor had prescribed sedatives: 'Do sit down, we are quite alone. Brenda has elected to go to the cinema.' Against her will her mind dwelt on an image of Brenda in the cellar, cobwebs lacing her hair, and Rossi, hands trembling, tearing her newspaper to shreds. I will rip you to pieces, she thought; and her hand flew to her mouth as if she had spoken aloud. Beyond the romantic dreams, the little girl waiting to be cuddled, it was power of a kind she was after. It is not so much that I want him, she thought, but that I would like him to want me.

Slumped dripping upon the carpet, she gazed into the

glowing mantle of the fire and rehearsed a small wistful smile.

Brenda waited a long time on the stairs to see who would arrive first. She had read Freda's note suggesting she go to the pictures – it was not so much a suggestion as a command: there was even 40p left on the mantelpiece. She must have been to the post office to draw out her savings. There was a bowl of salad on the landing and a lump of meat, curiously flattened and spiked with garlic, lying on a plate beneath a clean tea-towel.

At four-thirty the landlady came up from her basement flat on her way to her pottery class at the Arts Centre. She unlocked the back door and turfed the pregnant cat out on to the concrete patio.

'Damn thing,' she said, smiling at Brenda crouched on the stairs.

The cat, with sloping belly, stood on its hind legs and scrambled frantically with outstretched claws at the pane of glass. Freda said the landlady hadn't enough to occupy her time, going off to throw pots like that; but Brenda thought it was an inconsiderate judgement: they had never seen what she did on her clay wheel – she might have been another Henry Moore for all they knew.

'Shut up,' said Brenda when the landlady had gone. She peered through the banister rails at the cat running on the spot, irritated by the noise of its paws on the glass panels of the door.

She had come home exhausted from her thieving. Repeating her performance with the wardrobe, she had retrieved the brandy bottle from its place behind the lavatory bowl and buried it beneath the load of washing. When she wheeled the basket down the alleyway, she imagined the bottle breaking and the liquid trickling through the slats of woven straw and Rossi, like a bloodhound scenting the trail of alcohol, running up the street after her, nose quivering, black curls blown backward in the wind. He would call the police and have her arrested. Worse still, he might seize her by the arm and whisper insidiously into her ear his sensual desires, demanding she remain passive while he committed an offence in exchange for his not informing on her.

Outside the back door the agitation of the cat increased. She thought about letting it in, but she didn't dare: it might ravish Freda's steak and piddle on the lino. From behind the basement door came the piteous cries of its last kitten. The landlady had kept it, out of concern for the mother's feelings, but lately the cat had taken to biting it ferociously about the ears. Freda thought the animal ought to be sent to the vet and aborted: it was sheer wantonness to produce more offspring – she pointed out that if human beings had the same fertility rate a woman could have three hundred babies in five years. She said you'd need 2,000 eggs a week to give them all a good breakfast.

'I wonder,' said Brenda aloud, 'what the kitten thinks now its mummy doesn't like it.'

She wished someone would try to savage her every time she made a friendly gesture. She was just working out how happily she could exist, left entirely alone, when there was a knock at the front door. She wanted instantly to hide, but she knew it was no use, so she ran down the stairs with a fixed smile on her face, ready to leave immediately should it be Vittorio with his little silken Zapata moustache flopping above his mouth, or Freda back from her shopping. It was neither. It was Patrick in a shiny black suit and a clean shirt with a badly frayed collar.

'My word,' she said, letting him into the dark hall, 'you do look smart.'

His appearance alarmed her. He was so evidently out to impress, she would not have been surprised if, like a conjurer, he had whipped a vase of flowers from behind his back and presented them to her.

'Ah well,' he said, holding a canvas bag for her inspection, 'didn't I leave early to get me tools?'

She led him up the stairs, pulling faces as she went to relieve her feelings, sticking her tongue out at the brown-painted walls, telling him silently to drop dead and leave her alone. As they turned to go up the second flight of stairs, passing the cooker and the pungent slice of meat under its tea-towel, she was forced to smile at him and say insincerely: 'It is kind of you, Patrick, to give up your time.'

The bathroom had a geyser riveted to the wall above a large tub stained with rust.

'It's old,' said Patrick, looking at the four curved feet splayed out upon the cracked lino and the dust lying like a carpet beneath the belly of the bath.

Outside the window, open to relieve the odour of stale urine, the yard lay like a jigsaw puzzle, dissected by washing line and paving stone. On the back wall, above the black and barren stem of the rambling rose, stood a row of tin cans and broken bottles placed to repel small boys.

'That's it,' said Brenda pointing at the offending cistern in its bed of cement. Patrick climbed on to the lavatory seat in his sparkling boots and fiddled with the chain. 'It won't flush,' he said. Along the line of his sleeve appeared beads of plaster and a smear of rust.

'Your clothes –' began Brenda.

But already he was removing his jacket and handing it to her for safety. Lifting the heavy lid of the cistern, enough for him to get an arm in up to the elbow, he splashed about in the water, his shoulders raised so that she could see the elasticated top of his underpants holding his shirt in check.

'It's the ballcock,' he volunteered.

'Is it bad?' she asked, praying it was and he would give up and go home quick.

'Don't you fret. I can do it,' he assured her. 'Nothing simpler.

He jumped to the floor and looked in his tool bag for a spanner and a ball of string. She could see the damp cuff of his shirt clinging to the shape of his wrist.

'Look at that,' she said. 'You're ruining your shirt.'

'I was wondering,' he asked, his Brylcreamed head bent low. 'Would you have any objection to me removing me shirt?'

'I don't mind,' she cried, though secretly she did, and her eyes narrowed as she spoke.

Without his shirt, his hands and head looked as if they belonged to someone else, so red and full of blood against the white softness of his trunk. He had a nice chest, not at all pimply, with only a dusting of freckles between his shoulders. When he swung up a sleeve to release his shirt she glimpsed the bright ginger pit of his arm. Back he climbed on to the lavatory seat to probe about among the pipes and the plaster, and she hung his shirt on a nail behind the door and caught a faint smell of mould, as if he never aired his clothes but packed them half-dried into a drawer.

'Jesus, it's cold,' he said, feeling the chill air coming from the window.

'You could borrow my dressing-gown,' said Brenda, and he protested there was no need, the small pout of his beer belly overlapping the waistband of his trousers as he twisted to thank her.

'But you must,' she insisted, thinking there was very much a need; she couldn't bear to have him standing there half-naked. She went down the stairs, closing the bathroom door carefully behind her. She stood on the landing for a moment in case Freda had returned, but all was quiet and she crept like a thief into her room and went to the wardrobe, lifting out her dressing-gown, tugging it free from its place between Freda's dresses hung in polythene wrappers. The bottle of brandy, wedged in the folds of a purple cloak, fell on its side and rolled to the edge of the door. Thrusting it further into the recesses of the wardrobe, she ran back upstairs with her dressing-gown still on its hanger.

'That's nice,' he said, as she helped him into it.

Her fingers brushed the top of his arm rough with goose-pimples, and she stepped back not meaning to have touched him. The sleeves only came down to his elbows, and when he climbed back on to the lavatory the pleats of the bright blue dressing-gown swirled out like a skirt above his trousers and the gleaming tops of his Cherry-Blossom boots.

At first Vittorio sat on the chair by the gas fire where Freda had placed him, but she needed a man to open the bottle of wine he had brought and they both stood by the table, she fiddling with two glasses and he with the bottle between his knees to drag out the cork. He wore a black polo-necked jumper and a coat of real leather with two stylish vents at the back.

'It's strange,' she said, sipping her wine. 'I loved her, but we were not close.'

'Yes,' he replied, averting his eyes from her black nylon negligée, looking instead at the cheap utility furniture and the curved railings of the balcony reflecting the light of the street lamp.

'Are you close to your mother?' she asked him, not quite at ease, wishing almost he hadn't come. He said No, she lived in Italy.

'To your heart,' she persisted, touching her breast and looking at him earnestly. She was dreadfully hungry. The hairdresser had made her wait a long time and she hadn't had any lunch.

'Brenda has gone to the pictures to see *Super Dick*,' she told him, thinking it was a provocative title. She walked back and forth from the table to the window.

'I would have thought—' he began, but she lowered her head and he fell silent.

'Brenda's different from me,' she murmured. 'When I found her on the Finchley Road I did think—' and she too trailed into silence and left the sentence unfinished.

He had brought her a peach in a skein of tissue paper and she rolled the fruit between her palms.

'How kind of you,' she said, lifting his beautiful coat from the bed and taking it to the wardrobe in case she spilled wine upon it. When she opened the door a bottle of brandy rolled from the hem of her cloak and fell on to the nail of her big bare toe.

'Christ,' she cried, bringing her hand to her mouth and contracting her foot with the pain. 'Brenda,' she told him, voice husky with suppressed violence, 'never puts anything away.'

She stuffed the bottle behind the hanging dresses and

prayed he hadn't noticed. She didn't know how to broach the subject of food: if she mentioned the steak it might seem as if she were forcing him to stay – as if it were all planned. She poured herself out another glass of wine and gulped it down. He wasn't very talkative; he was making her do all the work. If he went quite soon she could eat the steak herself and the salad. She hadn't had time to make the garlic dressing, and how could she go out now on to the landing and start messing about with lemons. She was sweating from the pain of her crushed foot and the low rumblings of her empty stomach. Unable to contain herself, she nibbled a chocolate biscuit that Brenda had left on the mantelpiece and listened to the sound of hammering one floor above.

'I could do with some tea,' said Patrick, and Brenda had to nod her head as if it was quite all right and tiptoe down the stairs again.

She was always amazed at how seemingly-shy people constantly asked for things without a trace of embarrassment. How could she boil a kettle with Vittorio and Freda only inches away? The gas made a funny whining sound before the water warmed up, and Freda was bound to rush out on to the landing and create a scene. Hardly breathing, she lifted the kettle from the stove and was grateful that it was already half-filled with water. When she struck a match to light the gas, the ignition and flare of the sulphur were like the launching of a rocket. She trembled and dropped the matchstick on to the lino. Suddenly from behind the shut door, Freda began to sing. Under strain as she was, Brenda couldn't help smiling. Freda must have found the brandy bottle. She knew exactly how Freda must look at this moment, having seen her in the same state every Friday night after her visit to the theatrical pub. She would be standing poised like a Greek statue, head bent low so that her hair spilled about her face, one arm raised high in the air, one knee slightly flexed. Clicking her finger and thumb together, she would begin to glide in a small circle, round and round:

MacArthur's Park is lying in the rain . . .
I don't think that I can take it,
For it took so long to bake it,
And I'll never find the recipe again.

The kettle began its weird sighing.

'Oh-o. no. ohohoh,' roared Freda behind the door. 'Ohoho-oh-no-ohoh . . .'

She's always thinking about food, thought Brenda unfairly. She felt obliged to tell Patrick why the tea was lukewarm.

'You see, Freda's got a friend in and I'm not supposed to be here.'

He looked at her over the rim of his cup and didn't understand.

'A man. She's got a gentleman caller and she told me to go out.'

'It's your room,' he said. 'You've every right to occupy your own room.'

'Well, it's difficult. I quite see I'm in the way.'

She felt a bit foolish. She was conscious she was clipping the ends of her words and mimicking the way he spoke, as if she too came from the bogs of Tipperary.

'She expects you to leave your room if she has a fella in, then?'

'It's reasonable, I'm thinking,' she said, and blushed.

'You know,' said Patrick, 'I think a lot of you. No, honest to God I do. I don't like to think of her making a monkey out of you. Why, if I thought that, I'd throttle her – I would so.'

He had little freckles above the line of his upper lip so that the shape of his mouth was blurred. He put down his cup upon the side of the bath and wound a length of string tightly between his clenched fingers.

Vittorio had sat on the edge of the bed now, because Freda, undulating her Amazonian hips and pointing one foot at him, was moving more and more wildly about the room. He felt threatened by her size and the volume of her voice, and

44

there was a rim of dried blood along the cuticle of her big toe. He scuffed his suede boots beneath the iron frame of the double bed and kicked a book across the carpet.

'I read a lot,' said Freda, coming to rest beside him, the halo of her washed hair fanning out about her rosy cheeks. 'Poetry, Philosophy, Politics. The three pee's.' And she gave a loud, moist giggle.

'Such a lot of books,' he said, moving his feet about and shuffling more volumes into view, and she found she was telling him about Brenda and the way she couldn't bear they make contact in the night.

'She puts them right down the middle of the bed. It's frightfully inconvenient.'

'The books down the bed – ?'

'Well, you know – she doesn't want to run any risk.'

'Risk?' His eyes were wide with astonishment.

'Oh, come on – you know.' And she dug him quite painfully in the ribs with her elbow. 'It's like this,' she said, speaking very slowly, remembering the way Brenda talked to Rossi. 'She is afraid of life. She does not want to communicate. Know what I mean?'

The way he sat there so obviously not knowing what she meant, his handsome face solemnly gazing at her, filled her with irritation. 'What's the matter with you?' she asked. 'Why don't you relax?'

When he smiled she noticed there was a gap between his front teeth. It gave him the look of an urchin and minimized the sensitive modelling of his face.

'You've got gaps in your teeth,' she cried, and fell heavily against him.

He did kiss her then. He put his arm round her, and they thrashed about on the double bed. She clung to him and fastened her teeth in the woolly shoulder of his polo-necked jumper.

'I have to go to the toilet,' he said, struggling to his feet and striding to the door. She was left with a shred of wool stuck to her lip, alone on the rumpled bed. Another little drinky, she told herself, lurching sideways to the floor and

45

going to the wardrobe to find the bottle of brandy. She didn't want to be drunk. She didn't like the way things were going; but going they were, and she unscrewed the cap of the bottle and took a swig of the alcohol and wiped her mouth with her hand. The peach he had brought lay like a road casualty, squashed into the carpet.

When he returned she was aware that he was uncomfortable. He tried to make love to her but it didn't work.

'What's the matter?' she asked aggressively, pulling his hair quite viciously as he lay stranded upon her.

'The toilet,' he said. 'There are peoples in the toilet. I could not gain entrance.'

He was minus his shoes, but still wore his trousers and his jumper that was a bit chewed at the collar.

Brenda could hear knocking at the front door, growing louder and louder. She watched Patrick screwing a hook into the ceiling above the cistern.

'It's a bit Heath Robinson, isn't it?' she ventured, as he wound a length of string from the ballcock up to the hook in the plaster and down again to the metal eyelet of the lavatory chain.

She unlocked the bathroom door and stood listening. Freda had stopped singing, and the nurses on the ground floor had let someone into the hall. There was a murmur of voices, then silence, until she heard the dialling of the telephone. She couldn't hear the conversation, but quite soon the receiver was replaced and someone began to climb the stairs. Whoever it was halted outside Freda's room and rapped repeatedly on the panel of the door. She won't like that, thought Brenda, and then she heard the voice of her mother-in-law.

'I have come to see Brenda.'

'I'm afraid she is not at home.'

'I'll wait then.'

There was a pause before Freda answered, her voice charged with hostility. 'You can't wait. It's not convenient.'

'I shall wait none the less.'

Turning the curve of the stairs Brenda saw Mrs Haddon on the landing and Freda, hair dishevelled, straddling the threshold of the door.

'It's all right,' called Brenda. 'I'm here.'

'I want my photographs,' said Mrs Haddon, turning to face her.

'I want those pictures of my Stanley as a child.'

Brenda hadn't got them. She knew they were still in the kitchen drawer of the farmhouse, where they had always been, beneath the pre-war knitting patterns, but it was no use telling her so. Mrs Haddon was smiling firmly, nodding her head, the ends of her floral headscarf tied under the determined thrust of her chin.

'Go downstairs,' ordered Brenda. 'I'll get them.'

She frowned meaningfully at Freda who stepped aside, overwhelmed by her air of authority, and allowed her to enter the front room. Vittorio was standing at the foot of the bed, flushed and untidy. He wore a jumper that was unravelling at the neckline and he clutched his shoes to his breast. Brenda ignored him. She stooped to pick a book at random from the floor and went out again on to the landing. Mrs Haddon, a large plastic handbag at her feet, had obediently retreated down the stairs and was grasping the banister rail for support. Fancy her coming all that way from Ramsbottom, Brenda thought, all on her own on the coach in her nice camel coat.

'Here,' she said, holding out the book. 'They're all inside.'

They looked at each other. For a moment it might have been Stanley pleading to be understood – the same round eyes filled with perplexity behind the rims of the light-brown spectacles, the same wide mouth puckered at the corners. I can't say anything, she thought – nothing that's true.

Mrs Haddon lowered her eyes and bent to pick up her handbag. Freda, looking down, was taken by surprise at her appearance – such a pretty woman, rouge on her cheeks, a little tilted nose. She was taking something out of her bag and showing it to her daughter-in-law with an expression of eager expectancy that was quite touching to watch. From the way Brenda spoke about her in the past Freda had imagined her with cow-dung on her gumboots and straw in her hair.

'Why?' she heard Brenda say in a flat voice, not at all grateful – and then there was a scream. The sound, shivering above the well of the stairs, caused Freda to tremble from head to foot. She saw Brenda strike Mrs Haddon somewhere about the chest. The spectacles balanced on the bridge of the tilted nose jerked forward. A hand holding a gun swung upwards to save them. Brenda shouted: 'Don't –' and 'Why?' This repetition of an earlier question was spoken on a whining note. She cringed in her tweed coat, her red hair hanging limply upon the checked collar.

She's bent on destroying herself, thought Freda, and at that moment there was a small plopping sound as Mrs Haddon squeezed the trigger.

To see Vittorio hurtling down the stairs, his shoes falling to the carpet as if in pursuit, made Freda admire him all over again. A man was needed at this moment and he was there acting on her behalf, and it gave her a feeling of comfort and pride, for she was still trembling. At that moment Patrick the van driver, wearing a short-sleeved garment of powder-blue material, flung himself round the curve of the stairway and in two bounds leapt to join the struggling Vittorio below. How opportune, thought Freda, too shocked to question further. They held Mrs Haddon by the arms; they encircled her waist lovingly. Patrick reached for the gun raised high in the air and entwined his fingers in hers. They swayed, arms dipping up and down, as if energetically dancing. Brenda, standing apart in the recess of the ill-lit landing, put her hand to her mouth and bit the ends of her fingers. She was thin as a stick and behind her closed lids her eyes bulged, round as marbles.

'Pet,' cried Freda, launching herself down the stairs at last. 'My poor pet.'

The men, having manœuvred Mrs Haddon into the front room, placed her in the best chair by the fire with such force that she lost her balance. As she tipped backwards, her feet in their neat court shoes flew upwards, and she uttered a tiny cry of outrage. Vittorio, refined by his experience, put the gun on top of the wardrobe out of harm's way.

'That's my property,' Mrs Haddon said. 'I should be glad if you would give it to me.'

Vittorio stroked his drooping moustache and looked at Freda for instructions. She was standing at the window with Brenda in her arms, observing the police car in the street below, its blue light flashing as it cruised at the kerb.

'Look at that,' she cried. 'The police have come.'

'I phoned them before I came upstairs,' said Mrs Haddon. 'In case they were needed.' She half-rose to her feet and was thrust downwards again by the two men. They were not taking any chances.

'Answer the door,' commanded Freda, and Patrick did as he was told, running out of the room with the lapels of his dressing-gown falling open to expose his paper-white chest.

'We ought to make a cup of tea,' said Brenda, looking at Stanley's mother. 'She's had a shock.'

Mrs Haddon stared back without pity. 'I was only aiming at your vocal chords. You always talked too much.'

'Murderer,' cried Freda, quivering with indignation as she held Brenda to her breast. 'You should be put away.' All the same, she couldn't help being awed by the smart little woman on her chair, come all the way from the North by rail or coach, her handbag on her knee with her powder puff inside, her purse and her little black gun.

Two plain-clothed men and two in uniform came pounding up the hall. They asked a lot of questions about the old lady's relationship to Brenda and how she had come to be in possession of the pistol. Mrs Haddon said she only wanted to frighten Brenda to punish her for leaving Stanley and that she'd saved up her pension for three weeks to buy the weapon. She'd told the lady in the shop it was for her grandson and the lady had been very helpful. She gave her a card to go with it. She brought out of her handbag a paper target in red and black to show them.

They looked at it in silence.

After a time the uniformed policemen took her outside to the car, and the chief inspector and a sergeant made them all re-enact the drama on the stairs. Brenda felt silly holding out the book to the inspector, who was pretending to be Stanley's mother. She had to hit him quite hard on the chest and bite her lip in case she smiled. They wanted to know how they could contact Stanley and where he would be at this moment.

'At the Little Legion,' she said. 'But you better not ring there. He wouldn't like it.'

Freda shouted interferingly: 'Good God, he ought to be told. It was a gun she carried, you know, not a bunch of flowers.'

'It wasn't a gun,' muttered Brenda, 'it was an air pistol,' though she didn't know if it made any difference.

Freda told the sergeant that Brenda was separated from her husband. 'He gave her a very rough time in my opinion.'

'Quite so,' said the sergeant, looking at her and at Patrick still clad in the blue dressing-gown.

There was a knock at the door. The two young nurses from the ground floor, little white caps pinned to the frizzed nests of their hair, wanted to know if they could be of assistance.

'It's quite all right,' Freda told them frostily. 'It's just a small family party.' And down clumped the two girls in their crackling aprons and sensible shoes, desperate at being excluded from the excitement.

The police inspector asked Brenda finally if she wanted to make a charge.

'Definitely we do,' asserted Freda, and Brenda shook her head and said No, she didn't want to, thank you. Whatever would her mother say if she did and it got into the papers?

Freda didn't even bother to show Vittorio to the front door. She was tired now and grumpy. 'Get to bed,' she ordered Brenda, and she jumped between the sheets still in her negligée.

Brenda lay in the darkness unprotected by the bolster and

he row of books. She had tried to re-erect the barrier, but
Freda cursed and told her to bloody well stop messing about.

'He didn't make it,' said Freda, mouth crushed against the
pillow. 'He couldn't get into the loo.'

'Ah, well –' began Brenda, and thought better of it.

'I wonder if those were Maria's men in uniform?' mused
Freda.

'What men?'

'You know – Maria's men – in my cup.'

'They weren't on horseback.'

'No,' said Freda. 'You're right. What the hell was that
Patrick doing running round the house dressed like that?'

'He was just passing and I didn't like to say I was going
out.'

'You're barmy. What you see in him I don't know.'

'I don't see anything,' protested Brenda. 'He was just
mending the toilet.'

'Half-naked?' said Freda. 'You must be mad.'

When she closed her eyes the bed whirled round and
round. She had to force herself to concentrate on the outline
of the window pane.

Brenda said: 'I don't think she meant any harm. She was
just trying it on.'

'You need help,' murmured Freda. 'You're a victim. I've
told you before.' In the light of the street lamp the room
was glamorous and bathed in silver. The wooden foot of the
bed glowed like genuine mahogany. 'Isn't it nice?' she said.

'Stanley's mother must be furious she missed me. She
always hated being thwarted.'

Brenda wore a small gratified smile. She understood perfectly why Mrs Haddon had wanted to do her damage. Inside
her own brain she had on numerous occasions perpetuated
acts of brutality against friends and enemies alike.

'She needs putting away,' said Freda, beginning to fall into
sleep. 'You all need putting away.'

CHAPTER FOUR

For several days Freda was not herself. She suffered out
bursts of rage followed by long periods of silence. The rages
which were habitual, did not disturb Brenda as much as th
moments of moody reflection; she could not bear to witnes
her friend slumped on her beer crate or in the armchair b
the gas fire, deaf to all overtures. It was unnerving to liv
with. Freda was so fond of verbalizing her emotions. Sh
never brooded. Pain felt, or insults endured, made her th
more articulate. In adversity she saw the funny side. Sh
would spit out words describing in precise detail just hov
badly she was wounded, until her shoulders began to shak
with the burble of huge choking laughter that finally burs
from her.

She took to lying awake at night, counting the priso
bars of the balcony palings reflected on the curve of th
ceiling. She watched intently the plummeting bird of th
hanging lamp, the bunch of dried leaves in the mantelpiec
vase stencilled upon the gleaming paintwork of the door
When she looked out into the street it was bright as day
The lattices of windows, the lids of dustbins, the metal flank
of parked cars flashed in the moonlight and dazzled her
Brenda lay in darkness, the lower half of her face shot awa
– only the rim of her eyelids touched by light.

'What's wrong, love?' asked Brenda over and over. Bu
Freda, eyes glittering with fatigue, refused to tell.

She did go to see Rossi. She told him that if there wa
any more nonsense with Brenda in the cellar she would g
to Mr Paganotti and have him dismissed.

'Just because you're the manager,' she told him spitefull
'it doesn't mean you can wreak your vile will on Brenda.'

'I do not understand,' said Rossi, shrinking behind hi
desk littered with test tubes and sheets of litmus paper. 'Wha

is this wreaking? We only do a little fun.'

'Fun,' she thundered. 'Man, I don't think Mr Paganotti would call it that.'

He hated her. He clenched his chubby fists and scraped his wedding ring across the desk, stuttering his denials. He made the mistake of trying to humour her.

'You are a woman of the world,' he said. But she quelled him with a glance. 'Watch it,' she warned, her arms folded, her nostrils flaring, her silken face poised and tinted like an angel above the powerful wedge of her body.

He lowered his eyes, and back she strode to her bench and the quota of Nuits St Georges.

Maria was curious to know what was wrong, but Freda shook her head with an air of martyrdom, as if her burdens were beyond comprehension. She had thought Vittorio would never wish to speak to her again after that deplorable evening when she had drunk too much; but surprisingly he asked her several times if she was feeling better, if she was recovering, as if it had been she who had been shot at, for she had forgotten she was in mourning for her mother. He even wanted to take her out to dinner, but she refused. 'Later,' she told him, not caring to shut the door entirely. The thought of a visit to a restaurant, the clatter of knives and forks, the blaze of lights in gilt mirrors as they drank at the bar, filled her with panic. The effort of keeping her elbows off the table, her knees together, her voice down and delicately modulated, was beyond her. The scene on the stairs was imprinted upon her imagination; the inspector's request to know the particular relationship between the old lady and Brenda rang in her ears. Brenda was surrounded by people who claimed her as their own. Her father sent postal orders, her mother wielded power by the headings of her letters – 'Darling' meant Brenda was in favour; 'My Dear Brenda' spelled disapproval, as did the absence of those inked kisses penned at the bottom of the page. Stanley's balaclava hung on a hook behind the door. Under the bed, face down in the dust, lay a wedding photograph of Stanley arm in arm with Brenda, her dress smudged with flowers. His mother had ridden across the country with a gun to prove she was related by marriage. And Freda had no one to call her own except the distant aunt in Newcastle.

'I must be ill,' she thought, 'bothering about such trifles.'

She went to the theatrical pub to be among people who understood, and was unwise enough to tell her version of Mrs Haddon on the stairs. She performed modestly and with seriousness, rolling a cigarette nervously between finger and thumb, and was distressed at the wild hoots of mirth that interrupted her narrative. She joined in the laughter – tears squeezed from the crinkled corners of her eyes – but she was hollow inside.

Brenda tried to expiate the trouble she had caused. She said how well Freda looked, how revolting Patrick appeared in his overalls – that hair, those badly bitten nails . . .

'You're no oil painting yourself,' said Freda, cutting her short. She was grateful to Patrick. After all, the lavatory was mended, even if every time the chain was pulled the hook tore plaster from the ceiling. Brenda carried her coffee to the bench and lifted bottles whenever they were needed.

'Leave off,' cried Freda sharply. 'I'm not an invalid.'

Stanley telephoned later in the week. Rossi called Brenda into the office, Freda marching behind with a slender bottle of Spumanti still in her hand, and he fled from his desk like a rabbit and busied himself at the brandy shelves.

'I can't come down, Brenda,' said Stanley. 'I can't leave the hens.'

'I don't want to see you,' mouthed Freda.

'That's all right,' said Brenda. 'I don't think there's much point.' She was already flattening her vowels to accommodate him.

'What's that you say, Brenda?' he shouted at the end of the wire.

'There's no point you coming down.'

'I can't come down, Brenda – not with mother in hospital. They're sending her home in a day or two, Brenda.' He would keep naming her, as if there was some confusion in his mind as to who she was.

'What's he say?' asked Freda, tweaking her severely on the arm, and she said: 'They've put his mother in hospital.'

'Who's there, Brenda?' he said. 'Who's that with you, Brenda?'

'No one. What's the weather like your end?'

'You what, Brenda?'

'Nothing,' she said. 'I've got to rush now.'

She replaced the receiver quickly and tried not to think about him. She knew he would continue to stand by the windowsill for several seconds, calling her name down the dead wire, scratching his head when he finally realized she was no longer there. He would go out into the yard, the doves with pouting breasts asleep on the guttering of the barn roof, and stand with mackintosh bunched about his waist and relieve himself on the nettles by the ruined pig-sty. At the splattering of water on the leaves, the doves would rise with the flutter of wings and scatter the bantam hens pecking in the dirt.

'You're not firm enough with him,' reprimanded Freda. 'You're too soft with him.'

'I was always waiting for him to come in or waiting for him to go out,' said Brenda, as if to excuse herself. She was curious to know why Freda had defended Patrick earlier in the day. 'You never used to have a good word to say about him,' she reminded.

'I don't see the point,' Freda informed her, 'of denigrating anyone for the way they look. Certainly he's not of your class – that's one thing. But the state of his finger nails has nothing to do with it.'

She looked at Brenda so contemptuously, at the neglected growth of hair and the parched texture of her skin, that Brenda brought her hand to her mouth to cover the front tooth which was chipped since childhood.

Nevertheless Freda sought out Patrick before she left the factory and told him to leave Brenda alone.

'There are things,' she said, finding him in the loading bay, the chill air empurpling his face, 'that you can't know about. Far be it from me to tell anybody how to live their

55

life, but – ' and she waggled a rigid finger at him, 'you should
look for someone of your own age.'

'I like her,' he said stubbornly, ignoring his fellow worker
shifting crates of wine on to a lorry. 'I'd swing for her, that
I would.'

'I hope,' said Freda, bewildered by his headstrong declar
ation, 'it won't come to that.' And she turned on her heel
and went to collect Brenda who was in the washroom rinsing
out the sponges for the morning.

'I can't understand it,' she said. 'Whatever did you do to
that Patrick?'

'I only let him mend the lavatory,' exclaimed Brenda.

She looked so plain and dowdy in her shabby coat and
worn shoes that Freda smiled. It was ridiculous to think of
her as a *femme fatale*. Neither Rossi or Patrick would be
described as the catch of the year – unlike Vittorio with his
noble birth, his beautiful moustaches and his expressive
brown eyes. In only two days' time, on Sunday – for Mr
Paganotti was too stingy to allow them a day off work – they
would go on the Outing and picnic together under the trees
discussing where he might take her for dinner. She would tell
him how depressed she had been, how lonely. Looking at
her reflection in the mirror, her face appeared fragile and
tinged with silver. She felt the beginnings of restoration.

That night Freda slept more peacefully. At dawn she was
awakened by the sound of rain pattering thickly upon the
roof. The noise increased in volume and she sat up to look
out of the window, the hem of the white sheet sliding to the
folds of her belly, and saw a troop of horsemen flowing
along the river of the street. Drowsily she admired, as if in
a dream, the elegant khaki riders, the swelling calves of their
legs bound in puttees, the rows of mustard-coloured hats
bobbing up and down as they cantered toward the cross-
roads. She didn't move, she didn't blink an eyelid – after-
wards she thought she might have cried 'Hurrah' or tossed
a rose from the balcony – and they were gone, the stylish
riders and the taffeta-brown horses beating a tattoo on the

crest of the road.

It was all going to come true – she knew that now: the journey by land and sea, the uniformed men, the white dress with flowers at the waist. Perhaps they would live in a flat in Hampstead and have drink on the sideboard, meat in the fridge and Mr Paganotti to dinner once a month. After they were married she and Vittorio would visit the house-proud aunt in Newcastle and litter the hallway with their pig-skin luggage. She would drop her engagement ring into the glass bowl on the dresser for fear she tore the skin of his back when she held him in her arms. She would smoke in bed and spill talcum powder upon the rug. What disorder she could create with her paper hankies, the Cellophane wrappings of her cigarette packets, the pointillistic pieces of confetti still trapped within her garments! Auntie would have to lump it. In the summer, staying at his parents' castle outside Bologna, she would open the shutters in the morning to let in the sun and shield her eyes from the blue surge of the sea sparkling beyond the dusty line of the olive trees that his father owned. Brenda could come too, if his mother had no objection – and why should she, surrounded by her grand-children, her lovely bouncing bambinos gurgling beneath the lemon trees?

'You do look well,' said Brenda, propped up on the pillows, a plate of porridge balanced on her stomach.

'I am well,' cried Freda, already dressed, sweeping about the room with the transistor radio held to her ear.

She couldn't wait to tell Maria about the soldiers on horse-back.

'You're right,' she said, clasping Maria's hands in her own and dancing her round the cardboard boxes.

The sky was so overcast it was almost dark. The little naked bulbs hanging from the ceiling glowed like small red stars. Outside the row of windows the rain fell heavily and began to stain the concrete wall of the chip-shop.

Brenda thought Freda must have been dreaming. She hadn't heard anything, and what was a troop of horsemen doing at that hour of the morning in the middle of the city?

'Exercising the animals,' explained Freda jubilantly, 'before the traffic got going.'

'But we've never seen them before.'

'We've never been awake at that time.'

'I have,' said Brenda gloomily, thinking of the times she had watched the first streaks of the dawn appearing above the rooftops of the grey houses.

Now that Sunday was so near, Maria had begun to wonder what she might wear on the Outing. She had found a frock in Mr Paganotti's boxes. She pulled it out from under the bench and draped it across her portly body, waiting for Freda's opinion. It was made of silk, with a pattern of miniature daisies on a band round the hem of the skirt.

'Haven't you got anything of your own?' asked Freda dubiously, looking at the plunging neckline and the absence of sleeves. 'It's winter, you know.'

'Certainly I have nothing,' Maria said, and she whirled about with the hem of daisies flaring above the folds of her grey football socks, whooping with laughter and growing red in the face at her exhibitionism.

'I think it's very nice,' said Brenda.

'By all means wear it,' cried Freda, too happy to bring Maria down. And she looked about for Vittorio, anxious for him to know that her period of mourning was over. After all, she knew now that there was something in store for them both. The premonition of it was becoming stronger by the moment. She felt giddy at the thought of the future, and she longed to experience that shudder of excitement the sight of him might bring. She plunged down the steps into the basement, her large buttocks quivering in the brown trousers she had made herself, searching about among the barrels and the yellow containers, and calling his name for the pleasure it gave her. He wasn't there.

'He's in the office,' said Brenda, when she returned disconcerted to her bench. 'Him and Rossi.'

There were clients tasting the wine when she entered. A middle-aged woman dressed in black and a young girl in a grey coat with a velvet collar.

'Oh,' said Freda, 'I *am* sorry. I thought Vittorio was alone.' She looked at him tenderly, flashing messages with her eyes, and he hung his head as if suddenly shy in her presence. 'I wonder if I might use the telephone – to confirm the van booking for the Outing.'

She was all sweetness and light, her gestures theatrical and charming, her blue eyes wide with candour. The girl in the grey coat bent her head and studied the kid gloves on her lap.

'Later,' said Rossi. 'I am busy just now.'

He spread his fingers expressively and spoke in Italian to the middle-aged woman, who was staring at Freda with polite bleak eyes.

'Of course,' agreed Freda, 'how stupid of me. Do forgive me.'

It was fortunate for Rossi that she was in such a good mood. She seemed not to notice how eager he was to be rid of her. She lingered and postured, leaning against the shelves packed with pretty coloured labels. Finally she asked Vittorio if she might have a word in private. He went unwillingly to stand in the open doorway, and she laid her hand on his sleeve and said she was able to have dinner with him – that very evening if he wished. She smiled at him.

'Ah, no,' he said rapidly, trying to cover the sound of her voice by the breadth of his shoulders. 'I have made other arrangements.' And in spite of himself he gave a brief nervous glance over his shoulder at the group sitting about Rossi's desk sipping their wine in silence.

Freda made a gesture as if to touch his cheek, and he stepped backwards.

'Ah well,' she said, 'till Sunday, then. Tomorrow I will be preparing food for the picnic and washing my hair. I do want to look my best.'

As tall as he, she fanned his face with her breath and ruffled the fine hairs of his drooping moustaches. She fought to keep calm at this unexpected set-back. It hurt that he wasn't in the same frame of mind as herself. She was helped, however, by the sound of her heart palpitating in her breast, for all the world like the beat of horses' hooves.

'It is Madame Rossi,' informed Maria, when told of the women in the office, 'and her niece from Casalecchio di Reno.'

'Is it indeed?' murmured Freda, and she fixed her eyes on the office window and waited for the visitors to depart.

After a time a row of faces appeared at the glass and stared out at the factory floor, watching the workers at their labours. Deliberately Freda touched her lips with the tips of her fingers and blew Vittorio a kiss.

'You are awful,' complained Brenda. 'Rossi must be wetting himself, with his wife watching everything.'

'Rubbish,' said Freda. 'It should be obvious that Vittorio and I are close.'

There was an air of festivity in the factory. The men drank copiously from the barrel of wine and fooled with the women. They had never known Freda so animated.

At two o'clock, Salvatore, splendid in golfing shoes and a muffler of green silk, embraced Maria on her beer crate and received a blow on the cheek.

'Aye, aye,' she wailed, drumming her heels on the planking. 'They are mad for the Outing.'

She scrubbed at her face violently with her fist, to be rid of the moist imprint of his mouth. Salvatore, half-understanding her words, nodded eagerly at Freda and rolled his eyes with mock excitement.

Freda waited in vain for Vittorio to come and speak to her. She clung to the belief that she must not let go of him, that he was destined to be her true love, that he knew it too, only he had not begun to accept it. And yet, remembering the way he had recoiled from her outside the office door, she could not help but wonder. Was it the same for him? She shivered with the cold and drooped at the bench. She was dreaming now, rather than thinking clearly. She wandered among the ginestra bushes and the olive trees, and the cool white rooms of the flat in Hampstead. She rose in a giant jet above the toy blocks of the airport buildings and began her long journey over land and sea. Now and then she was aware of the dismal factory, the hum of machinery in her ears, the tenderly smiling face of the Virgin Mary high on the green-painted wall. Had she been alone she would have swung her head and crooned her love aloud.

Finally she was empty of images: no more pictures left in her head. There remained only an insatiable thirst for all the joy and glory of the good times to come, the life she was soon to know.

CHAPTER FIVE

Mercifully it was not raining. There was even a faint gleam of wintry sunlight. Brenda wore a black woollen dress, black stockings and green court shoes. Freda had hidden the tweed coat the night before; she insisted she borrow her purple cloak. Brenda didn't want to wear the cloak, but neither did she wish to annoy Freda. Protesting that it was too long, she draped it about her shoulders and looked down at the green shoes and an inch of stocking. Freda, in a mauve trouser suit, a sheepskin coat gaily worked in blue thread down the front, and a lilac scarf casually knotted at the throat, wrapped two cooked chickens in silver foil and placed them in the basket. There was a tablecloth embroidered in one corner with pink petals, a lettuce in a polythene bag, some french bread and two pounds of apples. In a small jar, previously containing cocktail onions, she had poured a mixture of oil and lemon and crushed garlic.

Having packed everything, she looked in her handbag and was dismayed to find she only had five cigarettes. She asked Brenda to lend her some money.

'I haven't any,' lied Brenda. 'You made me pay for one chicken and I bought the shampoo.'

It wasn't that she was mean, but she wanted to be prepared for disaster – the 40p in her purse was to get home if she was left stranded at the Stately Home.

Freda was livid. She kicked the basket roughly with her foot and threw herself on to the bed.

'How can I get through a bloody day like this on five ciggies?' she shouted.

'But it was your idea. You got us into it. I'd much rather sleep all day.'

'Shut up,' said Freda.

She looked at her wrist watch and noted the time. She had ordered the van for seven-thirty but had no intention of arriving at the factory before eight o'clock. It restored her good humour, prolonging the agony for Brenda, keeping her in suspense: she was probably dying inside with embarrassment.

'You shouldn't have spent your money on that,' said Brenda desperately, glancing at the table laid for two with the bunch of dried leaves removed from the mantelpiece and set in the middle of the cloth.

There were wine glasses too and a bowl of real butter, and stuffed olives on a saucer. God knows where they had come from, but two napkins, starched and folded, lay beside the blue-rimmed plates. She went to the window and stared out at the flats and the deserted balconies. At the foot of a tree a cat stretched and sharpened its claws on the bark. It shouldn't do that, she thought, and she heard Freda telling her not to hang about. 'We don't want your Patrick dying of a broken heart.'

It was five minutes to eight when they let themselves out into the street. The basket tipped on the steps and a loaf pitched to the ground. As Brenda carefully closed the front door, a huge gust of wind tore at the purple cloak and engulfed her in its folds.

'Christ,' said Freda, reaching for her hair, which was blowing in all directions, and retrieving the long thin bread from beside the dustbins.

At the corner of the empty street Brenda said: 'Honestly, Freda, I don't want to go. It's going to be awful. Couldn't I be ill or something?'

'Be quiet,' snapped Freda, pushing the basket ahead of

her, head bent against the gale.

A hundred yards from the factory the wind dropped and the sun came out quite strongly. Maria, a brown paper bag blown by the wind wrapped round her swollen ankles, ran to meet them with outstretched hands.

'There is a delay. We have no van. Amelio is not come.'

From beneath the hem of her working coat Mr Paganotti's frock, edged with daisies, hung a full two inches.

'My God,' said Freda. 'I might have known.'

She brushed past Maria and looked about for Vittorio. He was nowhere to be seen. The men stood in a row against the wall holding briefcases and carrier bags. They nodded and smiled, raising their wide-brimmed hats in greeting. It looked like a gathering of the Mafia – the street deserted save for the line of men dressed all in black, shoulders hunched, standing in front of the great doors of the factory, and the blonde girl taller than all of them, marching up and down with a face of thunder and a roll of french bread held like a sten gun under her arm.

Brenda tried to pretend she wasn't there, that she was alone at the top of a mountain. Just then Rossi, who had been poised in the middle of the road staring in the direction of the High Street, turned and saw her. Exuberantly he ran to her, his hostility to Freda forgotten in the joy of the occasion. How he had longed for this moment, this day to begin, driving into the countryside unaccompanied by his wife, as if he was an Englishman.

'Bongiorno, ladies,' he cried, 'Bongiorno.' Rubbing his hands together he positively jumped up and down on the pavement.

'What's going on here?' asked Freda officiously, folding her arms and looking at him with deep suspicion. 'I ordered the van for seven-thirty. Amelio should have been here a quarter an hour ago.' She had to bother about the details – the arrival of the van she had organized – even though she was sick to her stomach at the street empty of Vittorio.

Rossi shrugged his shoulders. 'The traffic, maybe. It is only a little waiting.'

'Traffic, you fool? At this hour?' She leant viciously on the wing of his Ford Cortina, and the car lurched slightly. 'I knew it,' she said to Brenda, as if the others didn't exist. 'I knew it would be a shambles.'

'It is only a little hitch,' reasoned Brenda, smiling at the row of workers ashen-faced with the cold.

Round the corner of the street came first Vittorio, then Patrick.

'There's no sign of it at all,' called Patrick, striding ahead in a belted raincoat and a cloth cap over his outstanding ears.

Brenda was surprised how like Stanley he appeared, in his mackintosh and his dark blue tie in a strangle knot at his throat.

Vittorio said something in Italian to Rossi, who shrugged again and consulted his watch. The men murmured and dug their hands deeper into their pockets. At the kerb stood the four small barrels of wine donated by Mr Paganotti. How old and worn, thought Brenda, are the faces of the men in the daylight. Indoors the lighted bulbs, the constant nips of wine, had tinged their cheeks with pink.

'Good morning,' said Vittorio to Freda. 'And how are you this wonderful English morning?'

He was mocking her. He was laying the blame for the weather at her feet. He was telling her how ridiculous she had been to conceive of this Outing.

'We're fine,' said Brenda quickly, smiling so hard that her jaw ached. Much more of this and her toothache would come on with the strain.

Vittorio was so beautiful in her eyes, his immaculate duffel coat fastened with white toggles, his chunky boots threaded with laces of bright red, that Freda was compelled to be off-hand with him.

'Oh hallo,' she said, as if she hardly knew him; and she turned her back. It annoyed her how confident he seemed. She was conscious that for some reason she had lost ground since the visit of Madame Rossi to the office.

'Are you not in a joyful mood?' he asked, and she pretended she hadn't heard.

'You are looking very nice,' Rossi told Brenda, looking at the purple cloak and catching a glimpse of black ankles above the shiny green of her shoes.

'Hmmmmph,' cried Freda, and she flounced several yards away.

'Is the great manager getting out of the wrong side of the bed?' asked Rossi unwisely. He was so happy himself he could not believe Freda was angry.

'Please, Freda,' begged Brenda, following her. 'Please behave.'

Brushing her aside, Freda returned to Vittorio. 'Look here,' she shouted. 'I hope you don't think it's my fault that the bloody van hasn't arrived.'

He raised his eyes at her outburst, and the men at the wall shuffled their feet and looked politely at the sky. How vibrant she was, always arguing and gesticulating, waving her loaf of bread like a battle flag in the air.

'She should get herself seen to,' said Patrick, gazing at her in disgust and admiration.

The sound of Freda's voice was suddenly drowned by a great bellow of rage from the street corner, at which appeared the missing Amelio on foot, shaking his fists and in the grip of some huge irritation. The men broke ranks and surged to meet him. A babble of voices rose in enquiry. What was amiss? Where was the van?

Amelio had risen from his warm bed at six to drive from his house in the suburbs to Hope Street. He had parked his small black car outside the factory and gone on foot to the garage off the Edgware Road to collect the van. They had told him that no such vehicle had been promised for today. He had remonstrated. He had pleaded. He had mentioned the name of Mr Paganotti. But there was no van.

'There is no van,' cried Rossi, turning to Freda.

'No van,' she echoed.

'No, no, no,' moaned Amelio, and he broke through the circle of workers and wrenched at the side door of his little black car. Rossi tried to reason with him. He placed an arm about Amelio's shoulders. He clutched him like a brother. He shook him until his own plump cheeks wobbled with passion and entreaty.

'What's going on?' asked Brenda, clinging to Maria, who was scarlet in the face with emotion.

'Amelio have a car. Salvatore and Rossi have a car. Nobody else. He want Amelio to drive us in the car to the picnic.'

'Oh God,' groaned Freda, crumbling the french bread into the gutter.

After a time Amelio freed himself from Rossi and got into the driving seat. He waved his hands at the window in a gesture of dismissal. Rossi stepped back to the kerb, and they all watched the black car slew in a half circle into the middle of the road and move towards the corner. It came to a halt, and then crawled cautiously into the High Street and vanished from sight.

'Poor bugger,' said Patrick.

The men stood for some moments not knowing what to do. A torn poster, advertising some long-finished event, whirled upwards and bowled along the road after the departed Amelio.

'Why can't we use one of the firm's vans?' demanded Freda.

'We cannot go in Mr Paganotti's business motors for a picnic,' reproved Rossi.

Freda felt discredited. She stood shaken, her scarf ends and her ash-blonde hair mingling in the wind.

'Give over,' she whispered to Brenda, who, dreadfully perturbed, was already picking her teeth with a matchstick.

After an interval of indecision, Rossi, seeing his excursion in danger, began to issue commands. He ordered Salvatore to the wheel of the red mini. He held up his right hand and indicated with his fingers that there was space for three. The men looked at each other and gripped their briefcases more securely. He propelled Brenda to the front seat of his Ford Cortina. 'In, in, in,' he urged; and she was bundled inside to find Vittorio in the back seat, where he had gone earlier to be out of the cold. They didn't speak. Brenda peered out of the window at Freda holding the mangled loaf to her heart. Rossi, skipping about frenziedly, and acting as if the street was on fire and must be evacuated immediately, motioned Freda towards the car. He held open the rear door, and she bent her head. As she made to enter, Vittorio vacated his seat and leapt out into the road.

'Bloody hell,' said Freda, white-faced and utterly demoralized, endeavouring to accommodate herself and the basket on wheels inside the cramped interior. The car sank on its axle.

'I wish I could die,' thought Brenda; and then again, 'I wish I was dead.'

There was a great deal of shouting going on in the street. A small boy on the far side of the road, intent on his paper round, stopped to stare. A face loomed up at the window of the Ford Cortina. Brenda unwound the glass, and Anselmo, in a slouch hat, brought his sad face on a level with hers and proceeded to kiss her, first on one cheek, then on the other. He went away, and his place was taken by Stefano, who contented himself with shaking her hand.

'You take my place,' urged Brenda, looking down at his hand lying like a little cold piece of cloth in her own. 'Honestly I don't mind in the least.'

'Ah no,' he said, 'you are young.' And he backed away clutching his carrier bag filled with bread and salami, the tears standing in his eyes.

Vittorio was arguing with Rossi and Aldo Gamberini, the overseer of the loading bay. They gripped him by the arm, one on either side, and attempted to drag him from the pavement. He resisted strongly. Rossi winked and grimaced in the direction of the parked car. He patted him playfully on the cheek as if to say 'Don't be a silly boy,' and Vittorio, finally submitting and followed by Aldo Gamberini, clambered sullenly inside the Ford Cortina. The vehicle rocked as he and Freda fought for leg space between the wheels of the shopping basket.

Outside there was an orgy of hand-shaking and leave-taking. Around the bonnet of the red mini the men clustered like tired black flies. Brenda could see Maria waddling up

67

the road in retreat, the hem of the silk frock bobbing against her calves. She ground her teeth in misery and stared hard at the picture of the Virgin pasted to the dashboard of the car.

At last Rossi flung himself into the driving seat.

'We are all right,' he assured them over and over, clutching the steering wheel bound in black fur.

As he looked into the mirror to make certain he had clear access to the road, he observed the barrels of wine being trundled towards the red mini. Out he jumped, waving his arms censoriously, and the barrels, all four of them, were transported to the boot of the Ford Cortina.

'Now we go,' he told the silent passengers, and he pressed the starting motor.

The small diminished face of Patrick appeared at the back window. He flattened his pugilistic nose against the glass and made frantic gestures to be admitted. Outside, the farewells of the dispersing workers rose in a continuous murmur like the sea.

'Go away,' bade Freda in a low voice.

He tugged at the handle of the door, the hen-speckled face beneath the peak of his cloth cap distorted with urgency. The door swung open and he tried to squeeze inside. Freda struck him repeatedly in the face with the french loaf and he fell backwards on to the pavement in a sprinkle of breadcrumbs. Brenda slumped as low in her seat as she could. She hadn't the heart to wave. She fixed her eyes on the silver ignition key, dangling from the lock, and the humble smile of the Virgin as she gazed at her bright pink child.

The engine roared into life. The car jumped away from the kerb and gathered speed, passing the homeward-bound men going in twos and threes to the tube station, shoulders bowed in the best black suits worn for a special occasion.

Rossi drove as if any moment he was about to be overtaken and sent home. He hunched his shoulders in his casual jumper and pressed his foot down hard upon the accelerator. He drove as if heading toward the Park and suddenly swung left into Monmouth Street, moving at speed past the barred windows of the army barracks and the rows of still-sleeping houses.

'Ah well,' he said, as if speaking to himself, 'it is only a little upset.'

There were few people up at this hour – an old man leaning on a stick, a girl in a caftan, an oriental gentleman wearing silver boots with high heels. Rossi took his attention briefly from the road to watch the girl and was forced to brake hard as the lights changed from green to red. Freda was flung forward in her seat and brought up sharp against the handle of the shopping basket. She said nothing, but her intake of breath was audible.

'Are you all right?' asked Brenda, turning in her seat; but Freda, massive in her sheepskin coat, had closed her eyes.

Beyond the rear window the red mini, bursting with passengers, came into view.

Brenda said: 'They must have been so disappointed – the others – going all the way home again.'

It haunted her: Maria in her silken frock, the prepared food lying unwanted in the black briefcases, the high hopes of the early dawn and the disillusion of the morning.

'They are used to disappointment,' Rossi told her philosophically. 'They have had their lives.'

He looked in the mirror and studied Vittorio and Freda huddled together. He spoke in Italian to Vittorio, but there was no answer. After a pause Aldo Gamberini said something to Rossi, who replied at length with much beating of his hands on the steering wheel. Brenda was glad she was wearing the enveloping cloak: at every gear change he brushed her thigh with his little finger curled like a snail.

She was surprised when she recognized Marble Arch ahead of them. Existing as she did between the bedsitting room on the first floor and the bottle factory down the road, she mostly imagined herself as still living somewhere in the vicinity of Ramsbottom – 'What am I doing,' she thought, 'in a car loaded with foreigners and barrels of wine?' In spite of herself she began to quiver with threatened laughter: sounds escaped from her in small strangulated squeals. Freda stabbed at her neck with her middle finger.

'What's up with you then?'

'I was just thinking about things?'

'It's nothing to laugh about.' But she laughed all the same, a great bellow that engulfed the car and made Rossi feel everything was fine.

'We are having a good time, yes? All is all right now?'

'Oh yes, we're having a good time all right.' And again Freda gave vent to a hoot of mocking laughter that caused Brenda uneasiness.

'I wonder how many fitted into the mini,' she said quickly to distract her, and Freda squirmed in her seat and peered out of the rear window.

'It's not there,' she said.

'Rossi,' cried Brenda, 'the car's not following.'

'It is all right. Just a little delay. They will catch up with us.'

'Those poor buggers,' burst out Freda, 'trotting off home.'

'Every Sunday,' said Vittorio, breaking his silence and lazily contemplating the great white houses of Park Lane and the glass frontage of the Hilton Hotel, 'my family go on an excursion to the sea-side.'

'Oh yes,' sneered Freda, 'we all know about your Outings. I suppose the maids run on ahead carrying the garlic sausages.'

He smiled tolerantly and stretched his arm along the back of the seat to touch a strand of her hair.

'Don't touch me,' she warned, though she was moved, and tossed her head in pretended annoyance. Brushing her coat with her fingers, preening herself, she showered breadcrumbs on to the floor.

'You hit Patrick,' said Brenda, 'with that bread —'

'He deserved it. Bloody fool.'

The glittering shops, closed for the day, flashed past the window. The blue dome of a Catholic church, emblazoned with a golden cross, leant against the white cloud-filled sky.

A row of well-dressed women, in fur coats and mantillas, linked arms and pranced in a line down the flight of steps.

'Where the hell are we?' demanded Freda, outraged by their red lips and their slim high-kicking legs. 'Where are we going?'

Rossi shrugged. 'It is a little surprise.'

He himself had no idea where he was heading, the original plan to go to the Stately Home had evaporated with the ordered van. He simply drove away from the city and followed his instincts. He only knew that Mr Paganotti lived somewhere near Windsor on the river and it was the countryside.

'I don't want to be surprised,' said Freda. 'I'll kill that Amelio when I see him.'

'Amelio is a good man,' defended Rossi, 'a good worker and a good father – '

'The bloody fool went to the wrong garage. It's obvious – '

Vittorio and Aldo endeavoured to explain.

'It is not Amelio's fault – '

'He tell me he went to the garage you tell him – '

'Maybe you tell him the wrong day,' said Vittorio.

'You have been a little upset lately,' Brenda said, and could have bitten her tongue.

'You make me sick, you do.' Freda hit her repeatedly between the shoulder blades. 'You're always so damn reasonable. A bit upset am I? What about your mother-in-law? Don't you think that's enough to upset anybody?'

'I meant your mother,' whined Brenda, trying to edge forward on her seat to be out of reach. 'The funeral – '

She pushed her hands over her mouth, and laughter spilled from her splayed fingers.

'I don't blame your mother-in-law trying to do you in. Never saying a word out of place.' Her voice rose as she mimicked Brenda: 'She locked me in the barn but I didn't like to say anything. I saw her going to kill the kittens but I didn't like to interfere!'

She thumped Brenda on the head. 'She was doing you a

favour if you ask me. You're sick.'

'Now, now,' said Vittorio holding her wrists in an effort
to restrain her.

They wrestled together on the back seat, Freda with her
lilac scarf crushed under one ear and Vittorio with his duffel
coat speckled with crumbs. Brenda felt sorry for Aldo. He
was red in the face with distress and bewilderment. She
winked at him to show she didn't mind, that it was only a
joke.

'Ah well,' said Rossi, 'we will have a little music.'

He turned the knob of the car radio, and instantly Tom
Jones was singing about the Civil War. 'I do rememb-bah . . .
a litt-al home-stead . . .' She saw the farm again, and all her
hysteria left her. She thought of Mrs Haddon dipping behind the hedge outside the kitchen window, a litter of kittens
in her apron, going to the stream to drown them. The cat
ran from under the rain barrel, its tail arched over its back,
hating the wet grass, shaking its paws fastidiously and
mewing in despair. When Mrs Haddon ducked under the
stile a kitten plopped to the ground, a black rat-like lump,
and the cat leapt and caught it in its paws and streaked off
across the field.

'She's so bloody reasonable,' she heard Freda say. 'You
can't get the truth out of her.'

'Rossi,' said Brenda, 'how can the mini catch up with us
if you don't know where we're going?'

At a garage near the approach to the M4 motorway, miracu-
lously the red mini did find them. Salvatore left the driving
wheel and accosted Rossi at the petrol pump. He indicated
the boot of the Cortina and the road behind them and waved
his arms about. Brenda couldn't see who his passengers were.
The windows were steamed up. She could only make out a
hand, flattened against the glass, and the brim of a hat. She
wished Maria could be with them – all those men and just
two women making for the wide open spaces. Freda, limp
after her outburst, dozed with her head on Vittorio's shoulder.
It amazed Brenda. She couldn't think why he hadn't cracked

Freda one over the ear and bundled her out of the car. She had called him a bloody Wop; she hinted his mother had never been married. Shaken but civil, he pushed aside the strands of tousled hair clinging to her moist lips and stroked her inflamed cheeks. Perhaps he liked it, thought Brenda. If she had reviled Stanley more, perhaps he would have stayed in to listen.

Rossi was telling Salvatore his destination was Windsor. Fresh air . . . a little jump out . . . a little game of football. He slapped Salvatore on the back and searched his face tenderly for traces of forgiveness. Salvatore hung his head and pointed his toe in the gravel.

Beyond the brown hedge at the side of the road a solitary cow cropped the grass. Salvatore wore a large fedora on his small head. Its brim stuck out above the padded shoulders of his coat and emphasized the elegance of his nipped-in waist. His hand bulged in his pocket.

He's making him an offer he cannot refuse, thought Brenda.

When Rossi came back to the car, he said, 'They are annoyed at having to pay the money for the petrol. They say it is not called for.'

'Well, they did pay 5op each toward the cost of the van,' reasoned Brenda and hoped Freda had not heard. She held her breath as the car nosed out into the thin stream of traffic.

It took some time to find the road to Windsor Park. When they left the M4, they could see the beige-and-grey castle, lapped by a pool of pale green turf, dwarfing the white houses of the town.

'We must be near,' said Brenda helpfully, as they crossed a bridge with a black swan perched on the water. The red mini had once more disappeared from the road. They came to the bowl of a roundabout, heaped with dahlias, and circled it several times trying to decipher which way the sign post pointed.

'There –' said Vittorio.

'No,' contradicted Freda. And they swung yet again around the small island of flowers until Rossi made his own decision and drove straight on. There were no ornamental gates as he had supposed. The pink-washed houses came to an end and the grey road cut through a green landscape spotted with oak trees. He slowed the car almost immediately and swung on to the grass verge. He bounded out into the fresh air leaving the car door swinging on its hinges.

'It's cold,' complained Freda, as Brenda climbed stiffly out to join Rossi on the grass sprigged with dandelions.

'This is the best place for a little jump out,' he cried, pointing eagerly at the woods in the distance, and the flat slanting top of a cut-down oak a few yards from the bonnet of the car.

'Good God,' Freda said. 'You don't believe in moving far from the main road, do you?'

She lumped her basket on to the verge and wrapped her sheepskin arms about herself for warmth, standing disdainfully in the shadow of the car. It wasn't as she had imagined. There were no lush valleys or rising hills saddled with yellow gorse. The land stretched flat and monotonous to the edge of the horizon. To the right was a clump of rhododendron bushes, a blackened oak splattered with the nests of crows, and a timber fence encircling a wood of beech and sycamore. Above her an aeroplane hung low, nose shaped like a bullet. Wings tipped with crimson, it shot in slow motion through an opening in the clouds. On the distant boundary stood the blue haze of a fir plantation, blurred against the white storm-tossed sky. Meanwhile the lorries, the private cars, the containers of petroleum, roared continuously along the road, shaking the parked Cortina on the grass and filling the air with noise.

'Now what?' she demanded. 'Now that you've got us here.'

Aldo Gamberini, his hat hurled from his head by a gust of wind, scampered across the Park in pursuit. His black trilby bowled to the foot of an oak and flattened itself against the trunk.

'Did you tell the others we were going to the Park?' asked Brenda anxiously. 'There must be a lot of entrances.'

'I say here, or maybe I say Windsor,' said Rossi, and he took out of the car a large white ball and bounced it up and down on the damp ground.

Vittorio caught it on the stub of his boot and kicked it high in the air. Hands deep in his pockets, he ran after it as it soared toward the clump of bushes.

'Wait, wait,' called Rossi, mouth trembling petulantly, as he tried to catch the tall young man now dribbling the ball selfishly ahead of him.

Trotting at Vittorio's heels, pestering, he tried in vain to regain possession. The two men ran in a wide circle with the muddy ball bouncing and rolling across the glossy windswept grass.

'Look here,' said Freda after ten minutes of this activity. 'I want to see the castle.'

She had been picking at the silver wrapping about the chickens, digging at the carcasses with her nails and licking her fingers. It was a quarter to eleven and there was no point eating yet – she would only be more hungry later on.

'You want to go?' said Rossi. He stopped running and stared at her in surprise, his cheeks rosy from his exercise with the ball, his suede shoes stained with mud. He spread out his hands expressively. 'We have only just come.'

'My dear man,' Freda informed him, 'the castle is redolent with History.' She wanted Vittorio to know how educated she was, to make up for the scene in the car. Also, she felt the need to be near a cigarette shop in case she gained the courage to ask him to lend her some money. 'Besides,' she said, indicating Brenda at the far side of the road, obsessively studying the stream of traffic, 'Madame won't settle until we find the others.'

'There is plenty of time,' protested Rossi. 'If they don't come in a little moment, we go.'

Freda kept her temper with difficulty. She pointed out that she hadn't intended to come here in the first place. She had planned to go to Hertfordshire. However, now they were here she was going to look at the castle.

With some spirit Rossi argued that it wasn't his fault if the plans had gone wrong. 'We take our chances,' he said mysteriously.

Vittorio decided to take Freda's part. He walked to the car and tossed the football at Rossi.

'Let's go,' he said.

How American he is, thought Freda, with his dashing moustaches and his baseball-type boots. The red laces trailed like ribbons in the grass.

She fitted herself into the back seat and allowed Vittorio to manœuvre the basket through the door.

'We are going?' asked Aldo Gamberini, his hat securely anchored to his head by means of a striped muffler tied under his chin. 'So soon?'

Rossi held the football to his chest. His mouth quivered. 'I want to play the games,' he said sulkily.

'Brenda,' shouted Freda. 'Hurry up.'

They positioned themselves in the car.

'There are little deer,' murmured Rossi forlornly. 'I think you like the little deer?'

'I will later,' assured Brenda. 'Honestly, Rossi, I do want to see the little deer.'

They drove out of the Park and back along the road to the flowered roundabout.

Freda thought the castle was wonderful. It towered above the main street, its beige walls curving outwards, the green grass studded with spotlights. She was reminded of a play about a Spanish family of noble birth that she had been in years before. She would have liked to have mentioned it but she had only understudied a rather minor part.

'Isn't it wonderful,' she breathed. 'It's so old.'

She couldn't wait to get out of the car and look at the dungeons. If she couldn't walk through the perfumed gardens with Vittorio, then maybe here where Henry VIII had danced with Anne Boleyn she could find an equally lyrical setting for the beginning of their romance. There were bound to be dark places and iron grilles, worn steps leading to cramped stone towers overlooking the countryside. There, above the Thames valley and the blue swell of the Chiltern Hills, he would, looking down at the small fields laid in squares and the ribbon of hedges, see in perspective how puny was the world and how big their love for each other. Accordingly she bustled out of the Cortina and lingered only momentarily outside the tobacco-scented doorway of a sweet-shop. Brenda insisted on writing a note in case the occupants of the mini came upon the deserted car and searched for them.

'After all,' she said, 'we have got the wine. I'll never be able to look them in the face again if they don't find us.'

'You never look anybody in the face as it is,' said Freda; and she drummed her fingers on the bonnet of the car, as Brenda drew an arrow on the back of an envelope, pointing towards the castle, and wrote: 'This way. We have just left.' She signed it 'Mrs Brenda'.

'You're mad,' Freda told her. 'You've got terrible hand-writing.'

All the same, Brenda felt more restful in her mind now that she had left some sign. She stood at various angles from the bumper of the Cortina to make sure her arrow was accurate in its direction.

Freda began to toil up the steep cobbled rise to the main gate, pushed from behind by Aldo and Vittorio.

'We are happy, yes?' said Rossi, and he attempted to put an arm about Brenda's waist. At that moment Aldo chose to turn and see if they were following, and Rossi jumped away, anxious not to be seen too intimate.

'He is my cousin.'

'He's a nice man,' said Brenda.

'He is very inquisitive.'

'Does he suffer from ear-ache?' she asked, looking at Aldo with the scarf wrapped about his head.

'It is a pity,' Rossi said, panting from the climb, 'that he fit in my car.' He cheered up and dug her in the ribs. 'Later,' he promised, winking at her encouragingly, and she did her best to look enthusiastic. If his happiness depended on her, who was *she* to offend him? He wanted his Outing, his day of escape. If the missing mini caught up with them, dis-gorging its quota of fellow-countrymen, then she would not be to blame if he was thwarted. 'It's not my fault,' she thought. 'I can't be expected to take any blame.'

'I've told you about that,' reminded Freda, turning to look at her.

'You shouldn't talk to yourself. It looks daft.'

Above them, carved on the gateway, mingling with the arms of Henry VIII, the Tudor rose blossomed in stone.

'Oh I wish,' cried Freda, 'we had a camera.'

She tripped forward in her purple trousers and gazed entranced at the toy soldier in his red tunic and rippling busby, motionless outside the guardhouse.

Salvatore spotted the Cortina with the envelope trapped on its windscreen at mid-day. There was a consultation as to what the arrow meant. Salvatore and his three passengers thought it peculiar that Rossi and the English women had entered the fortress, but the fifth occupant of the mini, not being Italian, said he understood. He borrowed a pencil from a traffic warden and wrote in English: 'We have gone that way too,' and signed it 'Patrick'.

Murmuring, the four workmen followed him up the hill and stood bewildered on the parade ground. Set at the end of the courtyard was a kiosk, and there was a thin stream of visitors buying tickets. On a pole above the State Apartments, a yellow flag, stretched stiff as a board, pasted itself to the sky. The soberly dressed men, searching for the lost remnants of their party, wandered beneath arches and descended steps. The wind rose in fury and blew them, jackets flapping, along a stone terrace above a garden. Wearily they climbed back to the parade ground and, urged by Patrick, joined the queue at the kiosk and paid 15p each to the attendant. Entering the doorway of a chapel, they removed their hats and shuffled past the alabaster font. They stared at the carved choir-stalls and the arched roof hung with flags, embroidered with strange beasts and symbols, heavy with tassels of gold. There were no candles burning, no crucifix, no saints bleeding and bedecked with jewels in the shadowy niches of the walls.

Bending their heads, they watched furtively the feet of

Patrick as he trod the tiled floor.

Freda had enquired and been told that the dungeons had all been sealed off.

'Off?' she repeated, outraged. 'Why?'

Rossi led her away, agreeing with her that it was preposterous.

'These things,' he said, 'how do we know why? What is the purpose?'

And he spread his hands and looked at her with such intensity of feeling that she was quite impressed by him.

He dreaded lest she fight physically with the custodian of the castle and have them ejected. Somewhere, beyond the main portion of the town, stood the family home of Mr Paganotti, set in gardens fragrant with falling leaves and dying roses. From every parapet Rossi leaned and searched the landscape for some sign of Mr Paganotti's existence. Once he had been promised he would be taken to the mansion – he had come to work in his best suit – but something had occurred to postpone his visit. He had waited in the outer office for Mr Paganotti to appear, until the secretary had come out shrugging her arms in her modish coat, and told him that Mr Paganotti had already gone. He did not allow himself to think that Mr Paganotti had forgotten – that was not possible. It was simply that he had so many responsibilities, so many cares – he had been summoned away with no time to explain. He had rehearsed how he would behave the following day when Mr Paganotti sought him out and apologized. He would raise his hand like a drawbridge and tell him no explanation was needed. Between men of business, excuses were unnecessary. He waited a long time at his desk, his hand flat against his breast, but even on the Friday when he went to receive his wages Mr Paganotti said nothing.

Freda was irritated when Vittorio corrected every item of information she gave him about the history of the castle. She understood, but she hated him for it. He was like her in temperament, conscious that he was mortal and determined to have the last word. She fell silent and was genuinely

79

upset that the State Apartments were closed.

'It's obvious,' said Brenda. 'If the flag's flying, she's here.'

A group of Americans, pork-pie hats jammed securely on their cropped heads, pulled out identical cameras from leather containers, and focused as one man on the statue of King Charles on his horse.

'She's in London,' said Freda.

'No here,' Vittorio said firmly, striding ahead of her like some monk of ancient times, the hood of his duffel coat about his head.

'If she wasn't here,' said Brenda persistently, 'we could look round her rooms and things. That's why it's closed.'

'Shut up,' Freda said. She didn't see it made any difference whether the Queen was in or out. Nobody actually saw her rooms. It stood to reason that State Apartments were separate. It wasn't as if they were going to catch her doing a bit of dusting.

The Gallery was closed too and the Dolls' House. 'Every bloody thing is closed,' she thought. 'I might as well give up.' The antiquity of her surroundings began to have a depressing effect upon her. What did it matter if Henry VIII had fallen in love all those times and lusted and eaten enormous meals? He was dead now and mouldered. She was further annoyed that she had to let Vittorio pay 15p for her to go into the Chapel. It was degrading, and it made it more difficult to ask him to pay for her ciggies. She stared gloomily at the carved gargoyles above the doorway, the swan and the hart and the dragon, and followed him inside.

The goggling tourists, the orange bars of the electric fires placed in strategic corners, robbed the place of solemnity. Above their heads, circled with motes of dust, stone angels spread their wings and folded pious hands.

'I want to go home,' said Freda, echoing Brenda several hours earlier.

'Isn't it smashing,' Brenda replied, fearful that Rossi had overheard. She sought Freda's hand and held it, trying to comfort her.

'That's Italian, isn't it, Rossi?' asked Freda. She pointed

at an inscription on the wall. 'What's it say?'

He studied it carefully. 'Ah well,' he said, 'it is the Latin.'

> Ave lumen oculorum
> Liberator languidorum
> Dentium angustia

'Hail bright eyes,' said Brenda unexpectedly. 'Sleepy liberator . . . bent anguish.'

'What's that mean?' asked Freda.

'It is the sufferers from toothache,' explained Vittorio; and Brenda felt it was an omen. Here, far from the farm and the absent Stanley, someone was caring for her teeth. Is it really, she wondered, trooping round the Chapel, holding Freda's hand in her own? Just thinking about it brought her down a flight of steps with a twinge of pain at the back of her jaw. She winced and stared intently at the warm pink stone ahead of her. They had come to the cloisters, a covered walk of meditation overlooking a patch of grass spread like a tablecloth. They were alone, the five of them, footsteps echoing on the ancient flagstones worn smooth by time.

'That's nice,' said Brenda.

'Let go of me,' hissed Freda. 'For God's sake, get lost.'

Seeing the deserted promenade lined with stone seats, she urgently wanted Rossi and Aldo and Brenda to go away and leave her alone with Vittorio.

Brenda didn't know what to do. She tiptoed self-consciously around the square and trusted that Rossi would follow.

'Lovely,' she murmured in a little more than a whisper. 'How old it all is.'

She went at a slightly increased pace along the southern flank of the cloister, relieved to hear the footsteps behind her. She turned left, fearful of coming back to Freda and found herself in the west wing of the Chapel. High on the wall was the fresco of a king with a white beard and eyes corroded by dampness. She paused and was joined by Rossi, his face pretentiously solemn as he stared upwards at the faded painting.

'Where's Aldo?' she whispered.

'He is somewhere.'

He made as if to retrace his steps, and she seized him by the arm. She had to think of something. Freda would never forgive her if they reappeared. After all she had ruined her assignation with Vittorio the night Mrs Haddon had called with her gun.

'I'm going to be sick, Rossi,' she said. And she pulled him down a dark passage set with little wooden doors and half-ran with him out into the open air and the cobbled forecourt. She headed towards a distant gateway, her arm in his, and found herself on a terrace overlooking a sunken garden.

'I'm weary,' announced Freda, and she flopped down on the convenient stone bench. Vittorio stretched his long legs and loosed the hood of his duffel coat. Small flecks of dandruff alighted on his shoulders. Aldo Gamberini, fretting at an archway, stared at the billiard cloth of grass. He cleared his throat. He wished he was working in his garden or helping his eldest son to oil his motorbike. After a moment he walked hesitatingly away in the direction of the Chapel.

'We will all be lost to one another,' said Vittorio.

'Ah no,' she said, 'not you and I.' And she leaned her blonde head on his shoulder.

'You and I,' he said, 'are birds of a tree. You do not let me be the man.'

Now that they were alone he did not mind talking to her freely. His impending engagement to the girl from Casalecchio di Reno was his own concern. At this distance, and with Rossi so obviously in pursuit of Mrs Brenda, he was content to lay his heart bare to the large English girl who treated him with such familiarity.

'I don't what?'

'You are always shouting. Giving orders.'

'I'm not.'

'You are never tranquil.'

'Oh I am,' said Freda. 'Don't you feel like a man?' And unfairly she laid her pale hand on his trouser leg and stroked his thigh. 'You and I,' she warned, 'could be something. I know about you.'

'What do you know about me?'

She brought her face closer to his until the hairs of his moustaches tickled the edges of her mouth.

'You see,' she confided, 'I'm not what I seem. I know I'm aggressive, but I'm not entirely. I'm surrounded perpetually by fools. Given the right opportunity, I could follow. If someone was strong enough to lead.'

She was staring at his mouth, her eyes veiled by the golden sweep of her lashes.

'Ah well—' he said, and his lips quivered.

'I need something serious. Something I can get my teeth into.'

He brought his hand protectively to the collar of his red jumper.

'I'm not fooling. I mean it for real. If I want something I go after it.' She looked at him boldly. He was mesmerised by her blue eyes, the creamy texture of her cheeks, her tinted nails moving softly across his leg. 'I'd do anything for you.'

'I cannot,' he said, 'be less than truthful with you. I have other commitments.'

She had not heard the concluding words of his sentence. She had heard him say he could not be less than true to her, and all else was drowned and deafened in the flood of joy that filled her heart and suffused her face with colour. He did love her. He could only be true to her.

'I will never let you go,' she breathed.

She clung to him and raised her lips to be kissed. An old man came out of a recess in the wall and passed them by. Clad in a long black gown bunched at the waist by a length of rope, he hurried deeper into the interior of the Chapel. Vittorio drew away from Freda and looked curiously at the open door.

'It is his home?' he enquired.

'Never mind,' she said. And she fondled his neck and twined her fingers in the tendrils of his soft brown hair.

It was easy now to be tranquil and happy and kind. She

was sickened by her unkindness to Brenda; she wanted everything to be lovely and safe, like the warm clasp of Vittorio's arms. She desired with sudden urgency to show him where she was born, where she had gone to school, a view from the top of a hill, the surface of a lake near her home, claybrown and pitted under rain. She wanted him to tell her that he too had seen a film years ago that only she remembered, that he too could listen with closed eyes to a certain melody. These few and fragmented reasons for believing love existed and could be unique stayed alive and sweet for perhaps thirty seconds in her mind – and faded as she looked beyond his shoulder, and the pale outline of his ear, and saw a line of black-suited men walking in single file along the opposite side of the cloister. Patrick, his cloth cap and pleasant face glimpsed in profile, strode in their rear. Freda pulled Vittorio's head down to her breast and closed her eyes. At that instant, Patrick, glancing casually across the square of smooth grass, saw them. He ran like a whippet beneath the pink arches and confronted her.

'You,' she said, stealing his thunder. 'How the hell did you get here?'

'Where is she?' demanded Patrick, his cheeks glowing like apples from indignation and the biting wind.

Vittorio bent to tie his shoe lace. He was worried inside; he felt that something had not been clearly understood. He dwelt fleetingly on the curved dark profile of Rossi's niece by marriage and wondered at Freda's formidable instinct. Was it possible she knew him better than he knew himself? Did she think she could take him by force?

'What have you done with her?' Patrick was asking.

Vittorio was not clear what was at issue. The Irish van driver was an unknown quantity. Nobody had explained what he was doing in the bathroom the night he had visited Freda. Maybe she had allowed him too to take liberties with her Rubensesque body. The remembrance of her billowy flesh and her grasping little hands pulling his hair made him giddy. He strolled casually away from the bench and appeared to be studying the grass.

Freda, seeing how he deserted her, was filled with hatred for Patrick. She wished the loaf of bread had been a broken bottle. Spitting, they faced each other, and Patrick held her by the shoulders.

'Help me,' she cried and twisted round to appeal to Vittorio, but he was no longer there.

'Swine,' she shouted, 'beater of women.' And she struggled with the Irishman, pinning him with her knee in his groin against the surface of the wall.

Vittorio, in the main chapel, waited for several minutes. He would have liked to have run for it, but Rossi had disappeared and he was next in order of seniority. Mr Paganotti would have expected him to do his duty. After an interval, Freda, quivering with anger, swept round the corner.

'What sort of man are you?' she raged.

'Sssh,' he said, fearful of the reverent tourists and the black-garbed priest climbing to kneel in prayer.

'He hit me,' she said. 'Where were you?' Her eyes blazed reproachfully.

'I do not want a scene.'

He turned and made for the exit, conscious he was a coward but terrorized by her loud voice and the strength of her arm.

Salvatore and his party were hurrying forlornly down the hill toward the car. But for the wine in the boot of the Cortina, so generously bestowed by Mr Paganotti, and the money they had already contributed to the Outing, they might have headed for home. It was just possible that Mr Paganotti might enquire if they had enjoyed themselves, and how could they disappoint him? They could not imagine what had happened to Patrick. One moment he had been ushering them forward and the next he had vanished into the shadows. He had abandoned them. They called his name softly, but there was no answering voice. Gino, an elderly man who had been once to visit his son in America and never forgotten the experience, said it was a sign of the times. 'Such a hurry they are in.' Speed and violence and a lack of consideration.

He shook his grey head and looked up at the North tower, as if Patrick might be seen clambering inconsiderately about the battlements. They trotted down the hill and huddled inside the interior of the mini and watched the women outside in the street.

'Please don't,' Brenda was begging, her teeth chattering, her back against the wall of the parapet.

Beneath her, the sunken garden, heavy with late-flowering shrubs, heaved in a spasm of wind. Rossi, his hands inside her cloak, his black curls blown over his forehead, took no heed.

'I am warming you,' he said, and he nipped her skin between his fingers and gobbled the tip of her reddening nose. She was looking foolishly at him and grinning toothily. He cound not understand why she was so friendly to him and so resistant. It was torture to him. He respected his wife. He did not wish to break the sanctity of his marriage vows or lower himself in the estimation of Mr Paganotti, but what was he to think when the English girl allowed him so much freedom? If he took no advantage she would think him a cissy. Perhaps Mrs Freda, with her apparent contempt for men, was indeed the true woman, open to advances.

Beneath them, the massive rhododendrons pitched under the scudding clouds. A ray of cold sunlight, salmon pink, washed over the grey stone. Across the valley, the beech trees with stripped trunks paled to silver.

'Look,' he said, 'how beautiful it is.'

She escaped from him and hugged the stone parapet and leaned as far as she dared, her thin hair hanging about her cheeks, and wished she was down there among the plump yew hedges, walking the paths littered with fallen leaves and the red berries of rowan. She thought of the commercial traveller who had stopped to give her a lift when she was going into Ramsbottom to buy groceries. In vain she said she was married, that her husband was big as an ox. He inveigled her out of his car and bundled her down beneath the bridge, his big feet snapping the stems of foxgloves, and panted above her. She wished Mrs Haddon had done her job properly, had put an end to this aimless business of living through each day. She squeezed her eyelids shut, but no tears would come. Rossi was behind her now, the muzzle of his face worrying her hair.

'Does Mr Paganotti live in a very big house?'

'Ah yes. He is a very big man in business.'

'What sort of a house?'

But he would not be put off. He dug his ferret teeth into her neck and redoubled his efforts.

Perhaps Freda was right. She was a victim, asking to be destroyed. With any luck Rossi would manœuvre her to such an extent that she would topple from the wall and be dashed to pieces. If ever I get out of this, she vowed, I will never be friendly again, not to anyone. Please God, send someone.

At that moment she heard a voice torn by the wind and saw Aldo Gamberini propelled along the terrace like a black angel, his arms flapping like wings, the cloth of his trousers whipped into folds about his prancing legs.

Rossi spoke to him heatedly. He clenched his fists and berated the cellar worker. Aldo Gamberini hung his head and seemed near to tears.

'Stop it,' said Brenda. 'The poor man.' And Rossi stalked away as if not trusting himself to say more, and returned abruptly, face sullen and voice harsh.

Severely reprimanded, Aldo followed them through an archway on to the parade ground and slunk down the cobbled hill. At the bottom he made to enter the red mini but Rossi would not allow it. Overcome with emotion, Aldo sank into the back seat of the Cortina and unwound the muffler from his head. His hat, limp over his collar, drooped like the ears of a whipped dog.

There was no contact between the two cars; no horn blowing or festive cries. Salvatore hesitated to remonstrate with Rossi – he looked so thunderous and out of sorts.

At last, through the gate at the top of the hill, came first Freda and then Vittorio. They walked separately, shrouded in emotion, until Freda stopped and asked Vittorio for something. He felt in his pocket and counted coins into her hand. He climbed into the car and it was agony for Brenda, faithful to her vow of half an hour earlier, to keep silent. She watched Freda enter the tobacco shop and reappear snapping the clasp of her handbag shut.

CHAPTER SIX

Freda laid her embroidered tablecloth on the ground, and it flapped upwards immediately and threatened to fly into the branches of an oak tree. She knelt on her elbows, bottom raised in the air, and told Brenda to help her. Between them they anchored the cloth at its four corners with the basket, the cooked chickens, the bag of apples and a convenient stone. The men were shy of placing their provisions on the cloth. They held tight to their briefcases and carrier bags and sat self-consciously on the grass. Stealthily – for hours of stalking each other about the castle had given them an appetite – they tore pieces of bread and chewed salami.

'For God's sake,' entreated Freda, 'put your food all together.'

She was like a matron, starched and encapsulated in her stiff sheepskin coat, ordering them to take their medicine. They did as they were told, heaping the loaves of bread and the fat lengths of sausage in front of her, and munched in silence.

Some children ran through the grass and stood at a distance looking at the barrels of wine perched on the slaughtered oak.

Freda served Vittorio first. 'Have the best part of the chicken,' she urged. 'Go on, have the breast.'

Brenda looked at the ground. Freda handed her a shrivelled portion of the wing and a piece of skin. I want chips, thought Brenda, in this weather.

'Come, come,' called Rossi, smiling at the children and

gesturing toward the food.

Freda scowled, and the children scattered and ran to the parked cars.

The morsel of chicken stuck in Brenda's throat. She longed for a mug of hot tea. 'It's nice here,' she said, and scoffed a hunk of bread and looked up at the road for signs of Patrick. Freda had said he had gone home. It didn't seem possible – he hadn't said goodbye.

Freda recollected that there was a safari park nearby. She said it would be nice to go there later in the afternoon. 'You know,' she said impatiently, 'it's a park full of wild animals.'

'Wild animals,' repeated Rossi. 'You are thinking of the little deer?'

'No I'm not. I'm thinking of the little lions and the little tigers – wandering around free, not in cages.'

The workers watched first Rossi then Freda, eyes flickering hopefully back and forth in an effort to understand.

'But it is dangerous,' said Rossi. 'We will all be running.'

'In the car, you fool. We go in the car and they're outside wandering about.'

Rossi liked the idea, once he felt it would be safe. He translated rapidly to the men, who murmured and looked at each other in wonder. They eyed the stretch of grass and the parked mini as if measuring the distance they might have to run.

Gino, whose son had gone to America, refused to eat communally. He had deposited his carrier bag in a pew in the chapel and forgotten to reclaim it.

'For God's sake,' bullied Freda. 'Feed, you fool.' And she thrust into his hand a yellow scrap of meat.

He shook his head politely in denial and turned his face to the wind, the unwanted food lying on his palm.

Vittorio ate heartily. He enjoyed Freda's salad and the dressing in the bottle. He put his bread on a paper plate and saturated it with oil. She watched the juice run down his chin and his fingers slippery with grease. She was repelled by his unabashed vulgarity, the common way he wiped his hands on the grass.

The wind slowly abated, the sky cleared and the sun shone. A dozen cars slowed to a halt and lined up on the grass verge. The men were warmed and revived. They filled their celluloid cups with wine and stretched out on the ground. Too polite to speak in their native language in front of the English girls, they remained monosyllabic.

'Stick this,' said Freda at last, when she had eaten her fill, and she rose to her feet and wandered away in the direction of the beech wood. She hoped Vittorio would follow. She was in a state of suspense as to his intentions. His declaration of true love, his betrayal moments later, had confused her. Still, she was not too distressed. The gradual turning of the October day from storm and cold to balm and mildness filled her with optimism.

Rossi wanted to play games, he tried to explain. He spoke in English to Brenda and in Italian to the respectful men.

'In the woods . . . a little jump out . . . you will count and we will hide.'

They looked at him without enthusiasm. He pointed at the woods and at Freda slowly perambulating round the perimeter of the fencing and covered his eyes coyly with his hands.

'We will hide and you will come to find.'

He jumped to his feet and urged Brenda to stand up.

'No,' she said. 'I want to rest.'

'Ah, never. We are here for a little jump out, yes?' And he pulled her quite roughly to her feet and she cried, 'No, no, later,' and sank down again among the dandelions.

The men averted their faces. They had had enough of finding and seeking. They knew well who would be found and who would be lost.

Rejected, Rossi went slowly to his car and returned with the stained football. He kicked it high in the air and the men lumbered to their feet and brushed down their clothes and ran about, eyes dilated and legs stiff from lack of exercise. Vittorio did not follow Freda across the park. Instead he discarded his coat and, luminous in a red jumper and trousers of black velvet, joined in the game. In contrast to

Rossi, who trundled, garments flapping, in a furious rush along the pitch, he ran elegantly with arms outstretched, placing the heel of one foot precisely against the toe of the other, as if balanced on a tight-rope. After a few moments several players stopped in mid-field and bent over, heads dangling, and fought for breath. If they felt the day lacked real splendour, they were too polite to declare it. It made no difference that the sky now drifted baby-blue above their heads – there were no village girls to dance with, no perspiring members of *la banda* blowing golden trumpets flashing in the sun; the wine balanced on the stump of the tree was contained in barrels of brown plastic. Digging their fists into their stomachs, the men jostled and stumbled together on the turf. They erupted into sly bursts of hysterical laughter as one or other of them, lunging too energetically at the flying ball, lost his balance and slipped on all fours upon the green grass. Patches of damp darkening their knees, and clumps of earth sticking to the soles of their winkle-picker shoes, they dashed back and forth between the oak trees.

Freda, lingering at the edge of the timber fence, watched Vittorio in his fiery jumper, flickering beneath the autumn leaves. She went very slowly round the curve of the fence and entered the beech wood. Singing in a slight acrid voice a song her aunt in Newcastle had taught her as a child, she started to march at a rapid pace, with swinging arms, along the path. After one verse, the bracken crackling beneath her boots, she stopped abruptly and listened. Faintly from across the park, now lost to view, she could hear the sporadic cries of the gambolling men, the drone of an aeroplane above her head and somewhere, deeper among the trees, the distinct noise of someone moving. She had the feeling she was being watched. She tried a few experimental paces further along the path and was sure she was being matched, step for step, by something invisible and level with her, screened by the stippled bark and the dying leaves of the beeches. She halted, and all was quiet. It was probably children playing Indians, stalking each other, unaware of her presence. Above her, the vapour trail of the vanished plane rolled wider and mingled with the clouds. Uneasily she continued along the path and tried not to feel afraid. She was nowhere near the safari park: it couldn't be a wolf or a runaway lion. There would be notices all over the place if she had wandered into the lion reserve. She paused and pretended to be examining the curve of a leaf. This time she saw the shape, human in form, of someone gliding behind the trunk of a tree. It's a dirty old man, she thought, relieved, but turned all the same and walked back toward the park. It would be funny if it was Mr Paganotti keeping an eye on them, watching to see if there was any hanky-panky going on in the forest. She wouldn't put it past him. He acted as if he owned his employees body and soul, handing out his cast-off clothing as if he was God Almighty.

A pebble, spinning from the bushes, glanced her cheek. Instantly she was filled with anger.

'Who the bloody hell did that?' she shouted, brave now that she was approaching the fence.

Another pebble, bigger in size, pitched on to the path a few inches from her foot. She went stealthily as a cat through the tangle of bushes, cuckoo spittle on her boots, and stooped to select a large stone from the undergrowth. Peering into the trees she flung it with all her strength into the gloom. There was a pattering of torn leaves, a thud, and an audible intake of breath.

'Serve you right,' she said and half ran, for fear of reprisals, round the curve of the path and into the park.

She trudged thankfully toward the running men and the tilted barrels perched on the oak table. She thought Brenda looked ridiculous, still wrapped in the purple cloak, attempting to kick the ball without exposing her legs. Freda said nothing, but she gave one of her mocking smiles.

'Do join in,' called Brenda. 'It's good fun.'

Her hair was messy and her ankles were braceleted with stalks of grass.

'Don't be absurd,' snapped Freda, and she lowered herself

on to the ground and propped her back against the stump of the oak.

She rubbed at her cheek with a piece of twig, trying to scratch it though not wishing to draw blood. Vittorio, pea-cocking across the pitch, hunched his shoulders like a baseball player and ran to her.

'Where have you been?' he asked.

She held her cheek and shook her head. He squatted on his haunches in front of her. Lip beaded with perspiration, his face bloomed like a rose.

'Ah, you have hurt yourself,' and he touched her soft cheek with one exploring finger. 'What has happened?'

'There was a maniac in the woods,' she said, 'hurling stones at me. I shouldn't be surprised if it was Patrick getting his own back.'

He found it difficult to understand. His eyes widened, and he waited for more words, but she bent her head and kept silent. She hadn't thought of the Irishman until this moment. Surely he wouldn't dare to chuck stones at her? Maybe it had been children. Perhaps some irate parent would come soon over the grass leading a bleeding child by the hand.

'Come,' said Vittorio caressingly. 'Be on my side. You play the ball game with me.'

He was challenging her, she thought, asking her to show her allegiance in front of the workers.

'I'm not keen,' she demurred, and he coaxed her to her feet, holding her hands in his. The men faltered and gave a few encouraging cries as the ball raced across the pitch.

'Why didn't you come for a walk?' she asked.

'But I cannot leave the men,' he said. 'It is not possible.'

Still entwining his fingers in hers, he dragged her some yards across the grass and then loosed her. She floundered as if in deep water among the sea of men, striking out, first in one direction and then another, in a breathless endeavour to intercept the ball kicked from side to side.

'That's it,' encouraged Brenda. 'Get at it, luv.'

She was in her stockinged feet, with one toe protruding

93

from a hole, hopping up and down with excitement. There was no goal-mouth to aim at – Freda wasn't even sure whose side she was on. She saw a row of black hats dumped on the ground and kicked out wildly with her boot. She missed and fell heavily on to her bottom. A faint titter began and died away instantly. Vittorio and Brenda, taking no heed, ran together, bumping and shouting after the bouncing ball.

Struggling to her feet, the tide of players rushing away from her, Freda returned, scarlet in the face, to the tree stump and turned the tap of the wine barrel.

Presently Vittorio came to see if she was all right. He looked at her spoilt face and disturbed hair.

'You want a little rest?' he said.

'My back,' she said abstractedly, as if it was an old burden she was used to bearing alone. She refused to meet his eye and winced bravely and bit her lip.

'Have you hurt your back again?' asked Brenda, leaving the game and looking at her anxiously. It seemed to Freda that wherever Vittorio went, Brenda followed. She stood very close to him, as if they were both united by their concern for her.

'Play on,' said Freda nobly, waving her hand selflessly at the make-shift football pitch, though she would have liked to catch Brenda a stinging slap across the face. She sank down with extreme caution on to the grass and closed her eyes.

'She's got a bad back,' said Brenda. 'It plays up from time to time. That's why she has to sit on a beer crate to do her labelling.'

'Perhaps a little sleep will do her good,' Vittorio said, as if speaking of his grandmother; and they went away together.

When Freda opened her eyes, her head turned resolutely from the happy team of workmates, she was astonished to see a row of horses at the boundary of the field, flowing along the blue line of the firs. She sat up, shielding her eyes from the sun, absorbed in the sight, touched by some chord of memory, and watched them turn from mauve to chestnut brown as they swerved, two abreast, away from the trees and began to canter across the park. At this distance they resembled an illustration she had seen in a war book, sepia-tinted, of cavalry on the march. They came nearer, the thud of hooves muffled by the grass, and she saw that there were three riders each leading a saddleless horse on a long rein, and they were no longer brown but jet black from head to tail with trappings of dark leather burnished by the sun. Now she knew who they were. She could see quite clearly the peaked caps of the mounted men, the mustard jackets buttoned at the throat. The game of football broke up. The workers flocked to the tree stump to refresh themselves with wine. They gazed in awe and pleasure at the animals and the proud uniformed men sweeping toward them.

'It's them,' cried Freda, getting to her feet and tugging Brenda by the arm. 'The other morning in the street – there were hundreds of them.'

She stared in recognition at the riders, red-cheeked and bright-eyed as if risen from Flanders field, the dead young ones come back to ride again.

'It can't be them,' said Brenda. 'We're miles away.'

Rossi, cherubic face beaming with hospitality, ran to the horses. The men reined in and slowed their mounts to a walk. Circling the oak, Rossi at their rumps, the animals snorted, flared nostrils lined with purple.

The soldiers looked down at the ill-assorted group, at the blonde girl in her sheepskin coat, the dishevelled black-suited workers, the paper cups strewn on the ground. Brenda, with her formidable nose in the air and an utterly misleading expression of haughtiness in her somewhat hooded eyes, spun on the grass like a bird caught in a net. She was terrified of the prancing beasts.

'You will have a little wine?' said Rossi, and he twinkled back to the barrel and turned the tap and rinsed out grass stalks from the cups, pouring the red wine on to the ground and refilling the beakers to the brim. Like a woman holding up refreshments to the liberating troops he smiled coyly and held out his arms. The three young soldiers dismounted. The horses pawed the turf and bent their necks, the clipped manes standing like a pelt of fur along the curve of their necks, the tails, dense as soot, swishing flies from their dark and steaming haunches.

The riders were on a training course from Aldershot. They were exercising the Queen's funeral horses.

'Funeral horses?' said Freda, eyeing the satiny flanks of the wicked-looking animals.

On great occasions, the soldiers explained, the death of military leaders, the laying to rest of Dukes and Princes, the Queen's horses, glossy black, pulled the gun carriage with the coffin on top.

'Of course,' said Brenda, remembering the death of Churchill. She looked discreetly at the rounded bellies, trying to ascertain what sex they were.

'Are they ladies or gentlemen?' she whispered to Freda. 'I can't see.'

'Geldings,' pronounced Freda, though Brenda was no wiser. 'You can't have stallions at a state funeral –'

'Why ever not?' asked Brenda.

'They're too fruity – it stands to reason. They might go wild and stampede down the Mall dragging the coffin at breakneck speed.'

'How awful,' said Brenda.

'They're very carefully trained. In Vienna it was an art in itself.'

Freda spoke as if she knew all about it, though in truth she had only ridden once, and that on a donkey at Whitby Bay when she was six years old.

The soldiers, young boys from country districts with soft burring accents, ate pieces of salami and crusts of bread washed down by the wine. In return, unasked, they offered the two women and one of the men a ride on the horses.

'Oh, no,' said Brenda instantly, 'I couldn't possibly – honestly. Thank you very much all the same.'

She stepped backwards, as if fearing they would fling her into the air by force and strap her in the saddle like some sacrifice to the gods of war. The workers, having been picked once in their lives by Mr Paganotti, hung back, not expecting to be chosen again. Vittorio made a token attempt to stand back for Salvatore, but it was not serious, and he and Rossi mounted. Freda, her delicate back forgotten, flung down her sheepskin coat and was hauled by two soldiers on to the large gelding, the plump curves of her purple calves echoing the rounded swell of the horses. Admiringly the men watched her swaying under the sky, her peach face shimmering amidst the golden strands of her blown hair. Vittorio, the red jumper giving a military air, rode at her side. The soldiers mounted their own beasts, the long guiding reins streaming out behind them, and began to canter slowly away from the pitch. Last went Rossi, hair clustered in damp ringlets upon his brow, bumping like a schoolboy across the neck of his horse. They rode through the air, level with the distant hills and the black fingers of the thorn trees, and Freda held an imaginary crop in her hand and tilted her chin imperiously at the sun. She was Catherine of Russia at the head of her regiment; she was Lady Barbara riding beside the young squire. Vittorio could not take his eyes from her; she was so majestic, so spendidly rooted to the black horse. She knew he was looking at her. She parted her lips, and a dimple appeared in her left cheek, and she thought, just at this moment we are one, you and I, only a little lower than the angels. They swept in a wide arc around the park, the scent of the firs mingling with the sweat of the horses, and turned at the curve of the timber fence, bending low to avoid the branches dipping in their path.

As they flashed past the beginning of the beech wood, Vittorio thought he saw someone in a peaked cap and a mackintosh running along an avenue of trees. For a second he imagined it was the Irish van driver, but he remembered that Freda had said he had long since made for home.

'Thank you so much,' said Freda graciously, as the horses stopped once more at the oak tree. 'It was so nice.' And she slid, light as a feather, it seemed, to the green grass and stood patting the nose of her horse.

Her knees began to tremble, her thighs ached; she had not realized how tightly she had gripped the belly of the saddleless animal. Exhilarated and unsteady on her feet, she smiled with childish satisfaction at Vittorio and said gaily to Brenda: 'Oh, you should have come. It was beautiful. It was so beautiful.'

They sat on the ground and lay in the sunshine. They drank thirstily from the barrels of wine. The soldiers, standing in their stirrups like jockeys, rode in a circle about the tree stump and made for the verge. Stepping delicately on to the gravel, the black horses swayed sedately toward the town, hooves clattering on the surface of the road.

'What did it really feel like?' asked Brenda.

'It was a bit like being on a swing,' Freda told her. 'Something gliding and rushing through the air. It was –'

'It didn't look like gliding. You were all jogging up and down like bags of potatoes.'

'Rubbish. I was –'

'You have ridden before?' asked Rossi.

He made it sound like an accusation. He was aware that he himself cut a poor figure in front of the cellar workers and was grateful that Mr Paganotti had not been present.

'Several times,' lied Freda, and she lay on top of her sheepskin coat, the wool curling in little fleecy knots about her purple limbs, satisfied, in spite of what Brenda had said, that she had been stunning in her deportment. She no longer needed to talk to Vittorio. For the moment she was sure of his admiration; she could afford to relax. She lay dreaming on her back, still experiencing the motion of the horse, the muscles in her legs trembling with fatigue. Behind her closed lids she indulged in fantasies: brandishing a riding whip, she leapt fences of impossible height and reached Vittorio, motionless in a meadow ringed with poplars.

The men went for little walks into the bushes or sat in the shade of the several oak trees and dozed. The parked cars had long since departed. The children, whining for sweeties, had gone from the grass. Brenda, not liking to lie down, in case she inflamed Rossi, propped herself on her side with her back to him and, leaning for protection as close to Freda as she dared, dug small holes in the soil with the tips of her grubby fingers.

After a time Rossi rose to his feet and wandered away in the direction of the fence. She watched his low-slung body amble across the park. He turned and waved, and she lowered her eyes and pretended she hadn't seen. Even at such a distance, his very presence in the landscape chafed her sensibilities. He was like some persistently hovering insect buzzing about her ears. She longed to swat him and have done with it. I ought, she told herself severely, to be able to speak my mind: I can't spend the next year or so running away from him. The thought of time lived as it was, spreading ahead of her – a long procession of days in the factory and evenings with Freda – filled her with gloom. She dwelt on the possibility of renting a room of her own: she would sit all day at the window without being disturbed, without having to respond. It occurred to her that she had escaped Stanley only to be dominated by Freda. Why do I do it, she thought, looking up abstractedly? And there was Rossi at the fence, fingers still fluttering in an absurd gesture of beckoning friendliness. Once and for all she would put him in his place. She jumped to her feet and strode purposefully over the grass. If he had been nearer it would have been easier. She had to walk quite a long way, and by the time she reached him she had been forced to smile once or twice and return his hand-waving. She trod on a snail and gathered it up on a leaf and brought it to him, cupped in her hands, to where he stood in tall grass and flowering weeds of red and purple.

'Poor thing,' she said, gazing with horror at the trail of slime oozing from its shell.

'It is the nature,' he assured her.

Impatiently he took her hand so that the leaf dropped to the undergrowth.

Anger revived, she asked snappily: 'What do you want?'

'We go for a little walk, yes?'

'No we won't.'

'We go now — come.' And he darted away as if he was a dog anticipating a flung stick and returned immediately. 'You come for a little walk?'

'I am not keen on a little walk.'

'A little walk is good. We see the little deer.'

'No.' She began to blush. 'I won't.'

He stared at her as if she was not well, eyes round with concern.

'Freda wouldn't like it.'

'Ah,' he said expressively, relieved that the problem was so simple. 'But she is not looking.'

'She may not seem to be, but she is.'

He looked at the mound of the blonde woman lying like a ripe plum on her coat of wool. 'She is having a little sleep.'

Brenda felt threatened. She had kept her eyes fixed on his in hopes of subduing the wild beast in him. Now, as he still advanced, she wavered. Her glance shifted to the trees beyond. She thought of the shadowy hollow to which he would lead her, the bugs in the grass, the spiders walking across her hair.

'No,' she said. 'You mustn't push me about.' Almost as soon as she had uttered the words she was sorry for them. She wouldn't like anybody to feel she was nasty. 'It's not my fault,' she said. 'I am thinking of you too. You see Freda said she would tell Mr Paganotti if you ever tried to interfere with me again. You wouldn't like that, would you?'

He couldn't deny it. Expressions of misery and doubt wrinkled his flushed face. 'She would tell things to Mr Paganotti?'

'Yes, she would — I mean, if she sees us going off, she would tell.'

'She would not dare —'

'Freda? She'd dare to do anything. She doesn't give a fig for Mr Paganotti.'

She had stabbed him twice, put in the knife and twisted it. The colour drained from his cheeks.

'It is impossible,' he said.

But she did not wait to hear any more. The longer she

stayed with him the more likely was it that she would find herself in another awkward situation. She turned her back on him and called over her shoulder: 'We should go back to the others. Freda will think there's something funny going on.'

The men had resumed the game of football under the captainship of Vittorio. His beautiful velvet trousers were crumpled now, his backside grey with dust from the ride on the horse. Brenda weaved her way between the sporting players and flopped down on the grass beside Freda. She was smiling.

'I did it,' she said.

'You what?'

'I told Rossi where to get off.'

Freda's eyes snapped open. 'Good for you. What did you say?'

'I said you were going to tell Mr Paganotti.'

'Whatever did you say that for? Why did you involve me, you fool?'

'But you said you'd tell Mr Paganotti. You said if ever – '

'You didn't have to tell him I would. You should bloody well have said *you* were going to.'

All the joy went out of Brenda's victory. She hugged her knees and despaired of doing the right thing.

'I thought you'd be pleased.'

'Why the hell should I be pleased? It's nothing to do with me what you get up to with Rossi.'

'You never said that before,' protested Brenda. 'If you hadn't been so nasty to Patrick he would have protected me.'

'Me – nasty to Patrick? That lout tried to hit me.' Freda was outraged at the recollection. She sat upright and combed her hair with agitated fingers.

'He never. You hit him with the french loaf.'

'Christ,' bellowed Freda. She jumped to her feet, snatching up her coat and waving it wildly in the air. A shower of grass and the gnawed bone of a chicken slid to the ground. 'He attacked me, he did – in the Chapel, he tried to punch me on the jaw.'

'I don't believe it,' whispered Brenda, though she did. She couldn't think what Freda had done to make the Irishman so violent. 'What did he say?'

Freda was staring across the field. Rossi and Vittorio, beyond the surging line of workers, seemed to be having an argument. Like dogs about to leap snarling into combat they padded in a small circle around each other. Vittorio's voice carried, harsh with anger, on the still air.

'What did he say when he tried to hit you?' persisted Brenda.

'Get off,' Freda said. 'What's it about? What are they saying?'

'It's foreign,' said Brenda sulkily.

Rossi had boldly asked Vittorio to take Mrs Freda into the woods. Though Vittorio was nephew to his beloved Mr Paganotti he would surely understand. Vittorio was appalled at the suggestion. His impending betrothal to Rossi's niece made such a thing out of the question: he was not a boy burning with lust, he was a man of honour. Rossi said nervously he was in bad trouble with Mrs Freda, and if she too could be disgraced then she would not be able to go to Mr Paganotti and report him for his conduct towards Mrs Brenda. Vittorio retorted that if Rossi had behaved indiscreetly with Mrs Brenda then he must take his punishment. He had dishonoured his family by his demeanour. He could not expect that others should lower themselves in order to protect him. Besides, he pointed out, the English women were different. No matter how many times he took Mrs Freda into the woods she would not feel disgraced, she would be flattered. She would run wantonly from under the trees and tell the whole of Windsor Park how beautifully she had been dishonoured.

Though Vittorio was nephew to Mr Paganotti, Rossi was bold enough to lose his temper and speak his mind. He shouted and shook his fists in the air.

The workers turned their faces to the sky, the ground, the flying ball, and missed nothing. Gino, the brother of old

Luigi, smote his forehead and murmured his disapproval.

'Whatever's going on?' fretted Freda. Her plump cheeks, childish with dimples and tendrils of disordered hair, quivered as she tried to understand what the two men shouted.

'Did Patrick do that to you?' asked Brenda, looking at the graze on Freda's face.

But she wouldn't reply. She fidgeted with the sleeves of her coat and longed to join in the battle.

'It's probably something to do with us,' said Brenda unwisely. 'Maybe he's telling Vittorio about you going to Mr Paganotti.'

'You're a bloody menace,' hissed Freda, convinced that Brenda was right. 'Why can't you stand on your own two feet without dragging me into it?'

'But you interfere all the time. You wouldn't let that lady borrow our room to play her trumpet in . . . You wouldn't let me talk to Stanley on the phone.'

'What lady?' asked Freda, bewildered.

'If you hadn't got rid of Patrick he would have stopped Rossi getting at me, and I wouldn't have had to mention Mr Paganotti.'

'Your teeth,' said Freda, 'are terribly yellow. You should try cleaning them some time.'

The workers, caught between two sets of protagonists, played all the more noisily. They wore themselves out kicking and shouting and running to the limits of the pitch.

Brenda saw Vittorio take hold of Rossi's hand. They're making friends, she thought, and she watched curiously as Rossi clutched his wrist. He seemed to be removing something from his arm.

After a time Vittorio stalked away from Rossi and left him alone at the fence.

'What's going on?' called Freda. 'What was that all about?'

He ignored her completely, running like a bull at the dribbling ball and giving it a tremendous kick in the air. It soared away and hit the branches of an oak tree and fell in a shower of leaves to the grass.

'You'll get nowhere talking to him like that,' said Brenda.

'He can't stand domineering women. You frighten him off.'

'How the hell would you know?' Pink with contempt, Freda put her hands on her hips and erupted into scornful laughter. 'You wouldn't know a real man if you saw one. Rossi and that bloody Irish van driver –'

'Stanley was a real man. Stanley wasn't –'

'Stanley?' The way Freda pronounced his name conjured up visions of a monster with two heads. 'You're not claiming he was a real man? Dead drunk all the time and –'

'Only some of the time,' corrected Brenda, in spite of herself.

'Good God! Any man that lets his mother run amok with a machine gun –'

'Please,' begged Brenda, 'don't shout.'

She didn't want it to go on a moment longer. The hatred she felt frightened her; she tried at all costs to suppress it. As a child her mother had terrified her with moods of violence, had ranted and raved and thrown cups upon the tiled kitchen floor. 'Come to Mummy,' she would say when the pieces of crockery had been swept into the dustbin, holding her arms out to the shrinking Brenda as if nothing had happened. The depths of suffering Brenda experienced and the heights of elation when Mummy returned, with tinted hair combed and nose powdered, had caused her for years to feel confused.

'Don't you like me talking about your Stanley, then?' said Freda. 'Is your Stanley not to be talked about?'

Brenda said: 'If you don't stop shouting at me I'll say something you won't like.'

'What?' Freda was curious. She stared at Brenda and asked almost tenderly. 'What do you want to say? Go on – get it out.'

Brenda had wanted to say that she looked like a long-distance lorry driver in the sheepskin coat, that she was a big fat cow, that she had wobbled like a jelly on the back of the funeral horse. She wanted to hurt her, watch her smooth round face crumple. But when it came to it, all she could murmur was, 'Sometimes you're very difficult to live with.'

'That's rich,' retaliated Freda. 'When I think what I have to put up with from you – you and your bloody bolster.'

'Well, there's things you do at night when you're asleep.'

'What things?' Freda was stunned.

'Well, you roll about and hold yourself –'

'I what?'

'You do. You cup your – your bosoms in your hands and jiggle them about.'

'I don't believe it.'

'You do – you do –'

'Well, what's wrong with that? I'm only dreaming. What's wrong with me holding – me – me –' but Freda couldn't go on. It was too intimate to talk about. Why do I do that she thought. Is it cancer, or lust, or what? Absently she began to walk in the direction of the rhododendron bushes.

'Where are you going?' called Brenda helplessly. It wasn't fair that Freda was walking away. It left her feeling wicked and burdened with remorse.

'As far from you as possible. And don't you dare try to follow.'

Freda's voice was subdued. She lowered her head thoughtfully and trailed her coat in the grass.

'They've been weeing all over those bushes,' warned Brenda.

But Freda never looked back. She pushed her way through the thick stems, fragments of mauve jumper and yellow hair showing between the dusty leaves, and disappeared from sight.

Rossi, biting his cherry-coloured lip in agitation, hovered at the fence, hands dug in his pockets, suede shoes scuffing the turf. He ignored Brenda who, curled up in her purple cloak, with cheek laid against the grass, was festooned with ties and waistcoats thrown down by the perspiring workers and touched here and there by points of silver, as cigarette cases and sleeve garters of expanding metal flashed in the sunlight.

Though drowsy, she kept her eyes fixed alternatively on the spiralling ball and the dense mass of the rhododendron bushes. Several times the ball thudded against the dark leaves and bounced backwards on to the pitch. Finally, after a spectacular kick by Salvatore, it hurtled over the bushes and dropped from view. Rossi, seizing his chance to re-enter the game, trotted forward and thrust his way into the foliage. There was a beating of undergrowth and snapping of branches. A small bird fluttered upwards. Propelled by invisible hands, the ball was flung back to the waiting players. She won't like that, thought Brenda. In the mood she's in she may very well punch him on the nose. Her eyelids drooped, and she drifted into the beginnings of sleep. Now that Freda was no longer alone she felt she could rest. The cries of the footballers receded. She was having a long serious talk with Freda – it was so real that she felt the drag of the grass as her lips moved – the earth rustled and crawled in the cave of her ear. She half woke. Vittorio was again holding Rossi's hand. He was attaching something to Rossi's wrist . . . The clouds whirled above her head . . .

When she fully woke and became aware of her surroundings, it was to see Rossi stumbling past her toward the car. He looked sick, as if he had a stomach upset from all the wine and scraps of food. She watched him climb into the back seat of the Cortina and close the door. She thought maybe Freda had said dreadful things to him, had told him he was ugly and squat and that his trousers didn't fit. She felt very tender. He was really a very nice little man. He loved Mr Paganotti. He worked from eight till six every day and he'd never stolen anything.

She got up slowly and went to the car, ready to pretend she didn't know he was there. When she came level with the window she thought for a moment he must have gone straight out the other side. He wasn't on the back seat. Puzzled, she stared over the roof of the car at the deserted field. On the edge of the horizon there was a machine with whirling blades stuttering across the grass. She watched it for several moments until a sound somewhat like the mewing of a cat came from the interior of the Cortina. It was Rossi, crouched on the floor with his knees drawn up to his chin and his arms covering his head, moaning.

'Oh dear,' she said, opening the door. 'What's wrong, love? Whatever's wrong?'

She had to pull his hands away from his face by force and was shocked at his expression of fear.

Scrambling into the car, she wrapped him within her arms, asking: 'What did she say to you? You mustn't take any notice. She never means what she says. She's kind really – you mustn't take it to heart.'

She examined his face anxiously for signs of assault. Though the skin under his watery eyes appeared bruised she couldn't be sure it was inflicted by violence. He spoke in Italian, teeth chattering, pouring out a flood of words, and she laid her finger to his lips and said, 'Don't, little lamb,' as if he were Stanley or someone she knew very well. 'It's no use,' she told him, 'getting yourself into a state. I've been through it myself – I know. Just try to forget what she said, try to block the words out.' And again, but rather more self-consciously, she pressed his head to her purple cloak and rocked him back and forth. Oh God, she thought, whatever did she say?

After a time he became calmer. He leaned his head against the seat and asked her what hour it was.

'I don't know,' she said, and she took his wrist to examine his watch. The glass was shattered and the time stopped at twenty minutes past four.

'Did she do that?' asked Brenda, but he remained silent. Fine rain began to spatter the windows of the car.

'Can't you tell me what happened?' she coaxed. 'Did she mention Mr Paganotti?'

A spasm of distress flittered across his face. He struggled from the floor and half-knelt on the plastic seating, nose pressed to the streaked glass, staring out at the clump of bushes as if expecting to see Mr Paganotti in his camel-hair coat advancing through the rain.

'Now that you're more composed,' said Brenda, 'I'll leave

you alone, shall I? I'll go and find Freda.'

'No,' he protested, gripping her by the arms, and she sank against him on the seat thinking he was his old self again and just as randy. She might even have submitted, if only to make him less unhappy, though she did wonder how they could manage in the confined space of the car and what she would say if the men ran in to be out of the wet. I could pretend it was artificial respiration, she thought and looked over his shoulder to see how the game was progressing. Out on the grass, standing beside the wine barrels, was a figure in a peaked cap and mackintosh.

'Patrick,' she cried and she thrust Rossi from her and opened the door and ran over the field.

The workers crowded about Patrick, curious to know where he had been. He was smiling, one eye elongated at the edge by a jagged cut beaded with blood.

'I don't think there's much left to eat,' said Brenda. 'Did you bring your sandwiches?'

She looked inside the shopping basket and disinterred pieces of bread and the cores of apples. She wished Freda would come and help. Even though she might be hostile to Patrick, she was awfully good at looking after people – in a jiffy she would have produced quite a substantial little meal.

'I'm not hungry,' said Patrick, looking toward the road.

Vittorio seemed uncomfortable in his presence. 'You have been in the town?' he asked, holding the ball to his red jumper and rubbing it up and down the flat curve of his stomach.

'In a manner of speaking,' Patrick replied, and stared at him without blinking for several seconds.

The men began to dress, knotting their ties at the throat, adjusting suspenders to concertinaed socks, taking out pocket combs and tidying their damp hair.

'Freda's gone to sleep in the bushes,' said Brenda, and looked about for her green shoes.

'I wouldn't disturb her,' advised Patrick.

'But we are all going to the safari park. It was Freda's

idea.' She pulled down the foot of her black stocking to cover her naked toe and struggled to keep her balance. 'Rossi's in an awful state,' she whispered, hanging on to Patrick's arm and wriggling into her shoes. 'Freda's had words with him. He's crying.' She looked briefly at the parked car.

'That's bad,' said Patrick. 'That's very bad.'

'I don't know what she said to upset him so much. I know she doesn't mean to be cruel. Honestly, Patrick, she'd give you the coat off her back if you needed it. It's just that she gets carried away.' She felt compelled to defend Freda. She herself had been sufficiently carried away to utter words that she now regretted. She should never have told Freda that she jiggled in her sleep. It was unforgivable. If you hadn't gone on about Stanley, she thought, I would never have mentioned it. She brushed down her cloak and walked towards the rhododendrons. I'm sorry, she said in her head. Don't be cross Freda. It wasn't true.

'I wouldn't wake her just now,' said Patrick. He laid his hand on her arm to detain her.

'Your eye,' she said. 'It's bleeding.'

She sought a way into the bushes, using her shoulder to prise apart the leathery leaves.

'Don't,' said Patrick, more firmly, and she looked back at him and thought he looked quite old, his face shadowy under the peak of his cloth cap.

'Freda,' she called, 'Freda, it's me.'

She struggled through the bushes, hands raised to ward off the bouncing leaves, and entered a clearing floored with tangled grass on which lay Freda, flat on her back with ankles crossed.

'Freda – we're going to the safari park.'

Freda looked disgruntled, her mouth sucked inwards. The blue eyes stared fixedly at the sky. Under the dark leaves her skin assumed a greenish tinge, the cheeks brindled with crimson and spotted with raindrops. For a moment Brenda thought she was weeping. Her painted nails, black in the shaded light, rested on the woollen swell of her stomach.

'Freda,' said Brenda again, and stopped.

Freda's eyes stayed open. A grey insect, sensitively quivering, dawdled on the slope of her thumb. Brenda knelt on the ground and touched the curled edges of hair turning brass-coloured in the rain. She couldn't understand why Freda's face, normally so pale and luminous, now burned with eternal anger, mottled and pitted with irregular patches of brown as if the leaves had stencilled rusty shadows on her cheeks. Only the nose was right, moulded in wax, the nostrils etched with pink. Where are you, she thought, where have you gone? She peered at her, trying to see what was different. It was as if somebody had disconnected the current, switched off the light . . . she'd gone out. Oh, she did feel sad then. Lonely. The terrible pious curve of her hands on the purple jumper – never again to jiggle her bosoms in the dark.

'Please,' she whispered. 'Please.'

She became very thoughtful, as if she had all the time in the world.

'Stanley,' she said out loud and watched a ladybird with speckled back laboriously climb a stalk of grass.

Freda's face, splintered into a thousand smiles and grimaces of rage, leapt at her from every leaf dipping under the onslaught of the rain. She laid her hand fleetingly upon the purple legs crossed on the grass.

'Little one,' she said, and rose to her feet again and left Freda alone.

CHAPTER SEVEN

In all the muddle of explanations and beginnings of sentences that were never completed, one thing remained clear. There was some reason, not yet clearly understood, for not fetching either the police or an ambulance.

Patrick had led Brenda to the car and ordered Rossi into

the front seat. He called Vittorio, who came slowly over the grass fastening his duffel coat and carelessly holding the embroidered tablecloth.

'There's been an accident,' Patrick told him when the door was closed. 'To Freda.'

Aldo Gamberini, shut outside on the grass, ran to the red mini to be out of the rain.

'But how?' asked Vittorio. 'What has happened?'

'She must have had a fall. When I saw her she was lying on her back. Her heart's stopped beating.'

Vittorio stared at the Irishman and then at the nape of Rossi's neck bordered with damp curls. He waited, but no one spoke.

'She is dead?'

'She is.'

'Her back? She is dead of her back?'

'On her back,' corrected Patrick; and Vittorio shook Brenda by the shoulder, and she said dully: 'No, it wasn't her back. You can't die of a strained back.'

'But we should–'

'Mr Paganotti–' whimpered Rossi. He continually rubbed the front of his shirt with the palm of his hand, as if fearing that *his* heart too might cease to beat.

'But we must–'

Brenda said: 'We can't be sure that–'

'How does he know?' said Vittorio looking at Patrick. 'He wasn't there. He say he was in the town. How can–'

'Rossi saw her. He went into–'

'I was searching for the ball. I came–'

'You have a bleeding eye,' said Vittorio, as though he had not noticed it before, and he made as if to touch the cut on Patrick's face. He had turned very pale. A tear rolled down his cheek, and he wiped it away with his sleeve. 'Where you get that wound? How you–'

Brenda was folding and refolding the tablecloth smoothing the petals of the pink flower in the right-hand corner. There was a smear of salad oil and a sweet smell of decaying apples.

'You and Rossi were arguing,' she said, 'up by the fence, and I had words with Freda. She went into the bushes.'

'I see her,' confirmed Vittorio. 'I think she go – you know – she need to – '

'No,' Brenda said. 'She was angry. She said I wasn't to follow.'

I can't, can I, she thought, not now? She hadn't dared to follow either when the soldiers had come to offer them a ride. How brave Freda had been, climbing aboard that monstrous funeral horse with its flaring nostrils and carved head. She hadn't looked like a sack of potatoes or a mound of jelly: she was regal in purple and motionless beneath the sky. She did mean it – it wasn't as if she thought Freda was listening.

'She had a graze on her cheek,' said Vittorio. 'She show me.'

Brenda asked: 'Did you really try to punch her on the jaw, Patrick?'

Vittorio suddenly recalled Freda's return from the beech wood. 'She tell me she saw you in the trees.'

They both looked at the Irishman in the peaked cap that shadowed his battered face.

'I never,' he said, 'and she didn't. It's not me you're wanting.'

Vittorio began to tremble. 'I do not want to think it – you see her first. You came out from behind the bushes in the middle of the football.'

'No,' said Patrick. 'He did – ' He tapped Rossi accusingly on the shoulder.

Through the tear-stained glass Brenda could see the red mini sluiced with rain. A faint sound of voices raised in song came from the interior of the car. Freda, she thought, must be getting awfully wet. What would the aunt in Newcastle say? Freda hadn't been home for years. She wouldn't tell her she'd been working in a bottle factory. If she was asked, she'd say she was a secretary, or doing quite well in commercials. Freda would like that. There were the theatrical set at the Friday-night pub in their second-hand clothes, but she didn't think they would hear about it. There wasn't anybody else. There wasn't even a photograph of Freda in the bed-sitting room. She'd never written her a letter or been on holiday with her or shared an adventure – only today and that had gone wrong.

She watched Vittorio and Patrick, heads bent against the rain, walking away toward the rhododendrons. She wondered if the arrangements for the van had been deliberately sabotaged. Perhaps it had been more convenient for Freda's plans that Rossi's car alone had been available for the Outing. It made for a more intimate group. It's a bit too intimate now, she thought, aware of Rossi beside her, still massaging his heart. There stole over her a regrettable feeling of satisfaction. She suspected it was normal in the circumstances. Superstitions were needed at a time like this. The wrong-doers had to be punished in some way. It was not to be wondered at that God had spoken. She remembered that Stanley and her own mother were great believers in the wrath of God. They both in their separate ways called upon him in times of stress and vengeance. 'God blast you,' Stanley had cried often enough when she turned her face to the white-washed wall to avoid his breath heavy with the scent of hops. 'My God,' invoked her mother when hearing of her engagement to the farmer she had met at a Rotary dance.

'What are they doing?' asked Rossi. 'Where have they gone?'

'They've gone to see Freda.' She looked curiously at his white face and his doleful mouth perpetually trembling. 'Tell me what she said to you in the bushes. I won't tell anyone, honestly.'

'Nothing – she said nothing.'

'I don't know what's the matter with me,' she confided. 'I don't feel very upset.'

They stared at each other. The pain in his eyes caused her own to fill with tears, but it had nothing to do with Freda. Every time she tried to concentrate on what had happened she was distracted by something trivial: the particular slant of a raindrop in the window, a piece of grass stuck to the rim of her green court shoe, the spread of veins in Rossi's hand as he gripped the driving wheel.

'*Santa Vergine,*' he murmured.

'Look at my shoe,' she said.

As she spoke, Rossi saw Vittorio and Patrick returning, running past the tree trunk toward the car. Vittorio slumped on the back seat and covered his face with his hands. He spoke in Italian to Rossi, who muttered and shook his head from side to side. Brenda thought she recognized the word 'Paganotti'. How they dote on him, she thought. Whatever will they tell him?

'We can't leave her there,' said Patrick, 'that's for sure. We'll have to bring her to the car.'

'But there's people you have to tell. We—'

'There's more to it,' whispered Patrick. 'You don't just drop dead—'

'Like doctors—'

'Not at her age—'

'She was in an awful state,' said Brenda, 'before she went into the bushes. Sometimes people have heart attacks when they get angry. I know of—'

'Never,' scoffed Patrick. 'Wasn't she always in a bad temper?'

The implication of his words reached her at last. For the first time since her return to the car she realized that Freda was dead out there in the park, never to live again. She experienced a prolonged bout of shivering followed by noisy intakes of breath and finally began to cry.

Twice Salvatore had come to the Cortina and been refused admittance. He made gestures outside the window and was waved away. He told his passengers that Rossi looked as sick as a dog and Vittorio too. They made jokes about it. They said it was the English women that had caused nausea, not the wine. They were in the mood to go to the safari park full of wild lions and tigers: they growled ferociously at one another and clawed the covering of the seats. Salvatore defiantly tooted his horn to remind the occupants of the

Cortina that they waited. In the meantime they sang loudly and helped themselves to the remainder of the Beaujolais that they had wedged into the back of the car when no one was looking. They watched the comings and goings of Patrick and Vittorio to the clump of bushes bowed under the rain and speculated as to what was going on. The Mrs Freda had drunk too much and was refusing to come out – they were enjoying her favours, the two of them; she had taken them both in her arms; even the weather could not damp her ardour. They were further amused when they finally saw her being helped out of the bushes – the interior of the mini rang with laughter. They stuffed mufflers into their mouths and watched pop-eyed the sight of Vittorio and Patrick unevenly balancing Mrs Freda under the armpits, the sheepskin coat hanging from her shoulders, her feet scuffing the ground; she had drunk enough for them all. Her head hung down limply; the dimmed hair, plastered to her cheeks was like a veil.

'We go now,' called Salvatore sticking his head out of the door as Mrs Freda was bundled into the back seat. Nobody answered. After some time he draped his jacket over his head and ran through the puddles to the Cortina.

'We go now,' he called, 'to safari park, yes?'

Rossi seemed not to hear. He caught a glimpse of Mrs Brenda leaning back exhausted against the front seat, face streaked with rain.

'Do you know the way?' asked Patrick opening the rear window, eyes obscured by the peak of his cap.

'Ah,' said Salvatore, 'we will follow the signposts. You follow me. I lead.'

And he ran enthusiastically back to the car and leapt inside, his coat still over his head, and started the engine. He reversed on to the verge, turned the car and drove deeper into the park.

Brenda couldn't turn round. She knew that on the back seat, secured between the bulk of Patrick and Vittorio, Freda sat like a large bedraggled doll, chin sunk on to her chest. They couldn't possibly drive all the way back to London like that, it wasn't right. She ought to be laid down properly and allowed to rest. There was such a thing as *rigor mortis*. She had a dreadful image of Freda, shaped like a sheepskin armchair, impossibly wedged in the doorway of the car. I do wonder where you are, she thought. It was so apparent to her that Freda was anywhere but in the back of the Cortina. Sheep, she knew, just lay and unravelled away, and hens were like burst pillow-cases – but not people, not Freda. She dwelt on the idea of something like an escape hatch under water, leaving her purple jumper and her hand-made boots behind. Even now she had beached on some pleasant island and was drying in the sun. Smiling, she glanced out of the window down a slope towards a collection of farm buildings set about with paddocks and gently rising hills. Through the branches of sycamore she saw an ornamental lake ringed with pink flamingos. It had stopped raining. There were people removing raincoats and furling umbrellas and a coach painted like a rainbow outside a cafeteria.

'What the devil is this?' asked Patrick. 'This isn't the way.'

He watched astonished as a mud-caked elephant appeared from beneath the trees and trod ponderously over the grass. The mini halted and Rossi braked; he sat quite still with his hands resting on the column of the steering wheel, unconscious of his surroundings.

Salvatore and his passengers spilled gawping from the car. They ran like children across the gravel and gestured at the dusty elephant beginning to sink to its knees in the paddock.

'Get out,' said Patrick. 'Go and ask what they're up to.' He sounded, but for his accent, remarkably like Freda.

Thoughtfully Brenda joined the workers gazing at the jungle beast settling into the ground.

'But we are out,' cried Salvatore, clutching at her arm. 'We are not confined. Where is the tigers? The little children is everywhere.' And she soothed him and said she thought perhaps elephants weren't dangerous, though privately she didn't like the look of the huge animal lying like a heap of ashes on the open field.

They had come to a children's zoo. There were kiosks selling candy floss and a helter-skelter greasily plummeting to a pan of sand. In a compound there were goats with tufted beards nibbling pink-lipped at handfuls of brown hay. 'Poof,' she went, inhaling a whiff of the white-washed stall and observing their stern yellow eyes fixed upon her.

They looked at donkeys and a calf splotched with brown lying woodenly beside a cow, and above them in the grey sky patched with blue an aeroplane swam like a duck towards the city. Aldo bought a postcard of a monkey eating a banana to take home to his children. 'To remind me of this day,' he told Brenda, grinning at her from beneath his weirdly buckled hat; and she ran conspicuous with swollen eyelids out of the gift shop and up a hill to a line of telescopes pointing like guns at the far-off park. She put her eye to the lens and swung the black cylinder in an arc, trying to find the cut-down oak and the piece of grass on which they had laid the tablecloth. It all looked the same. She couldn't tell one piece of ground from another: the trees stood identical, the road ran like a grey ribbon to the castle. She was searching for Freda. As she examined the magnified ground, she caught the Cortina enlarged at the side of the path and the blurred shape of Rossi slumped behind the wheel. Guiltily she ran down the hill to the car and said the men were determined to go to the safari enclosure. As she spoke, she closed her eyes to avoid confrontation with Freda.

'Sweet Jesus,' blasphemed Patrick, 'what are we to do?'

'We cannot tell them,' said Vittorio, 'we should perhaps turn round and go home alone.' He was desperate to be out of the car and away from his silent companion, yet fearful she would slide sideways at his departure.

'Wait,' said Patrick, 'I have to think. I have to decide what's best.' And he frowned and fingered the congealed cut at the corner of his eye.

There was no longer, Brenda thought, any possibility of turning back. It seemed to her that they should have driven hours ago to a hospital or a police station. A faint curiosity rose in her as to the outcome of their actions.

'Why can't we tell them?' she asked, watching Salvatore and his men licking ice creams at the side of the road. It was awful not being able to turn round and look at Patrick. She wanted to ask him things. She would have liked to know what he was afraid of.

He said: 'Be quiet, I'm thinking,' and he drummed his fingers on the back of her seat.

Aldo Gamberini came to the side window. 'We go now.' He pointed to the hill and the row of telescopes. 'The wild ones are that way.' He peered through the glass at the silent Rossi.

'Tell him it's all right,' prompted Patrick. 'Go on.' And he prodded Rossi, who stirred at last, listlessly and with great effort as if emerging from a deep sleep. 'Tell him we'll follow.'

The two cars moved down the road away from the helter-skelter and the dozing elephant. They passed a house behind a wire fence and an open air café. Above painted tables the multi-coloured petals of aluminium umbrellas still dripped from the rain. There were public conveniences marked 'Tarzan' and 'Jane', screened by saplings of silver birch and a toll box manned by a ranger in a boy-scout hat.

Vittorio paid the entrance fee – Patrick hadn't got any money and Rossi never moved. Brenda didn't think he was mean. It was just that he was in a state of shock and nothing got through to him. Since her own fit of weeping she was feeling much better, and she couldn't think why he was still so upset; he made her feel she was shallow for recovering so quickly. She wondered if it was safe to let him drive them through a herd of wild animals – they might all end up in a ravine.

The man in the toll box thumped the roof of the Cortina and told them to get out. 'You can't go through in that. Everybody out.'

'We can't get out,' said Patrick. The mini, revving its engine a few yards ahead, tooted an impatient horn.

'Why he tell us to get out?' asked Vittorio, gripping the

handle of the door in alarm.

'It's the sliding roof,' explained Brenda. 'It's not safe. The lions might rip it off.'

'Down there,' directed the helpful ranger, pointing further down the path at a rustic shelter thatched with straw. 'Catch your bus from there and park your car under the trees.'

They waited some minutes for the bus to arrive. They sat in a row with shoulders pressed together as if they had got into the habit of leaning on each other. Overhead the sky paled in patches leaving dark pockets filled with rain. The red mini waited for them, the men hardly understanding what was happening – they glanced curiously at the Cortina parked under the trees with Mrs Freda alone on the back seat.

The safari bus when it came was painted with black stripes like a zebra. It looked as if a whole pride of lions had hurled themselves at the rusty bonnet and ill-fitting windows and torn the tyres to ribbons. The driver was dressed in a camouflaged jacket of mottled green and a hat to match, one side caught up at the side as if he were a Canadian Mountie. When he opened the double doors at the back of the van, Brenda saw he was wearing plastic sandals, bright orange and practically luminous, and striped socks.

She nudged Patrick, who was edging forward to climb into the bus, and he stopped abruptly and asked 'What's up, what's wrong?' frowning and looking about in an alarmed way. The driver was beckoning her and she couldn't tell Patrick about the socks.

'Nothing,' she said, 'nothing.' And she clambered into the van and sat near the window.

'What's the matter?' asked Patrick sitting heavily beside her and tugging at her cloak.

'His shoes,' she whispered, 'and his socks.'

'His what?'

'Look at his feet.'

'For the love of God – what are you on about?'

She sighed and settled herself more comfortably on the wooden bench. The driver stretched out a speckled hand

119

shaking with palsy and started the engine.

'He's got Parkinson's,' she said. 'He shouldn't be driving a bus.'

Patrick was staring at Rossi's hand, braced against the green slats of the seat in front.

'Will you look at that?' he said, nudging her with his elbow.

'Not Rossi – the driver. Either that or he's over a hundred.'

'Do you see his watch?'

She looked without interest at the damaged timepiece. 'He broke it playing football.'

'Is that what he said?'

'He didn't say anything. I don't think he cares about his watch being broken.'

'When we got – her – up from the ground there was bits of glass – there was a piece stuck to her jumper – at the back.'

She listened and watched a dead fly, relic of a previous summer, quivering on the window pane. The bus rattled over ruts in the gravel path and bounced down a lane towards a metal fence covered with wire netting and patrolled by men with rifles.

'Oh God,' she said, 'do you think it's dangerous?'

'Will you listen to what I'm saying. Rossi was in the bushes with her before anybody else. His watch is bust. I told you – I seen the pieces.'

'What pieces?'

'Sweet Jesus,' he murmured. 'Your brain's addled with the shock. I can't make you see how serious it is. I can't get any sense out of that Vittorio and none out of you.' He sounded pained as if she had let him down. He stared gloomily ahead and watched the barricade slowly rising in the air.

'I'm sorry,' she said, 'but I don't seem able to take it in. I don't know why we didn't get a policeman. I don't – '

'For God's sake, will you think about me. I was seen. Wasn't I seen in that Protestant chapel having a barney with her?'

'But you said you didn't hit her,' she said primly.

'I didn't. I didn't lay a finger on her. She thumped me.

She pushed me into some hole in the wall and shut me in. I had a devil of a time explaining what I was doing in there.'

'She locked you in a hole?' Her mouth began to turn up at the corners – she couldn't help admiring the spirit of Freda.

'And she hit me in the eye with a bloody big stone.'

'Where?'

Vittorio turned and looked at them. He had dark circles under his eyes and his lashes were stuck together. 'What is wrong?' he hissed. 'Everyone is looking.'

'Ssh,' reproved Brenda. 'People are looking.' After a few moments she whispered: 'Where did she hit you with a stone?'

'In the woods.'

'You said you didn't go into the woods.'

'Well, I did. I was minding me own business, throwing pebbles at birds, and she chucks a bloody big boulder through the trees at me.'

'You shouldn't have thrown pebbles at birds,' Brenda said, shocked at his unkindness.

They drove through a field of ostriches who fled bedraggled at their approach and disappeared into some trees. It didn't look like a park. The grass was patchy and littered with lumps of dung; the leaves hung tattered from the branches.

'Isn't it messy?' she whispered in Rossi's ear, but he didn't reply. He was holding his wrist with one hand and hiding his shattered watch.

Brenda went pale. Beads of perspiration broke out on her temples. She struggled to open a window.

'You can't,' said Patrick. 'It's not allowed to open the windows. What's the matter with you?' And he stared at her ashen face and her pale lips parting as she fought for breath. 'Get your head down,' he ordered, and thrust her roughly towards the floor littered with cigarette ends. The blood pounded in her ears.

'Siberian camels,' called the driver, 'to our left,' and a murmur of appreciation rustled through the bus.

Brenda didn't faint. She revived in a moment and her

sensitive skin became blotchy with colour and she lay back deathly cold and very frightened.

'Bear up,' said Patrick. 'Take hold of yourself.'

She longed for him to take hold of her. She wanted to be protected. She wanted her hand held, but she couldn't be sure that it wasn't he that frightened her.

'What are we doing?' she asked, in much the same way as she had asked the dead Freda where she had gone.

'I'm telling you,' he said. 'I'm thinking. I've got to be careful.'

'But if Rossi – hurt Freda –'

'Do you think we'll get that bunch to split on him?' said Patrick scathingly, and he looked through the driving window at the red mini crawling between two ragged llamas. 'That lot will stick together. They'd be out of their minds with fear that Mr Paganotti would give them the sack. It'll be me that'll get it. They'll all swear that I vanished for hours and came out of the bushes with me eye cracked open.'

They had come to a second gate and there was a further delay. At a squalid ditch another batch of flamingos pecked at the bank and teetered on Belsen legs over the mud. They looked obscene, as if they bled all over.

'Was she bleeding?' she cried out loud, and Rossi twitched as if he had been stung.

'Sssh,' Patrick said. 'Her neck was broke.'

It occurred to her that he was cleverer than she had ever imagined. Worn at a jaunty angle over his large ears, the cloth cap she had previously thought common became stylish in her eyes. His face assumed a strength of character she had not noticed before. Vittorio, turning anxiously to look at them, moustaches lank, seemed insipid by comparison. Even the boots with scarlet laces appeared a shade affected.

'Sit up,' said Patrick. 'Pull yourself together.' He was altogether like Freda.

The bus passed under the second gate and traversed an empty field strewn with cabbages and turned sharply left into an arena of sand and dead trees, the whole fenced about with sheets of tin, dark green, dented in places and emitting a weird moaning noise as they vibrated in the wind. On hillocks of baked mud men postured holding whips, rifles slung upon their backs. Clothed in rags, the inmates squatted in the dirt and dipped bald heads and ripped their breasts apart. 'Vultures,' breathed the passengers and shivered in their seats. The men with guns stood motionless posing for photographs. The snout of a baboon was seen at the top of a slope. 'Ooooh' went the occupants of the bus, levelling cameras at the window and craning their necks to see beyond the slopes. 'Wait on,' said the driver, tooting his horn, and the armed guards ran up the hills cracking their whips. Barking like dogs, a horde of baboons, pink-arsed and hideous, swept over the ridge and bounded across the grey sand. They leapt to the top of a large rock and huddled together holding their young.

'Poor little things,' said Brenda. They were so ugly, so human in their aspect, so vicious in their glances.

'They'd have your guts for garters,' Patrick said. 'They'd tear you limb from limb.'

She thought of Freda sitting in the car under the trees, growing cold – it was a pity they hadn't let the Cortina into the reserve. Nobody would ever have known: a door jerked open, a quick shove – they could say her heart had stopped. She shivered at her own audacity. She tried to remember how Freda had looked when she cantered over the park on the black horse, but she couldn't. It was as if a chasm had opened between them, leaving Freda on one brink and herself on another. The gap was widening hour by hour. She felt like crying and asking someone for forgiveness.

'Listen,' said Patrick. 'You believe I didn't touch her?'

Her eyes were shining, the tears only just held back and she cleared her throat before she replied. 'Yes, I do. Don't be silly.'

'You're sure?'

'I am, I am.'

It was meaningless really, and he knew it. She had the kind of temperament that stopped her from being truthful. All the same, he thought he might persuade her.

'What we do,' he said, 'is to get her back to London and put her somewhere while I think how to make Rossi tell us what happened. In your room –'

'No,' she said. 'Don't do that.'

'For me.'

His face loomed over her; he bared his teeth like a baboon. He'd told Vittorio he had never been in the woods. She had heard him. He said he'd been in the town. He was so anxious they shouldn't go to the police . . . Freda had a graze on her cheek . . . He was looking at her imploringly. She wondered if he guessed what she was thinking; despite herself she couldn't help recoiling from him and pressing closer to the windows.

As they left the arena a solitary monkey leapt to the top of the slope and stood upright. Dangling a long thin penis like a scarlet lupin, it swung its arms in rage.

The lions and tigers were a disappointment. They lay in lusher pastures under the feathery branches of horse-chestnut trees and slept.

'They are not wild,' cried Rossi, and he unclasped his hands and banged on the window with his fist.

When they returned to the bus shelter, Patrick suggested they should all go for a cup of tea in the cafeteria. Aldo Gamberini tiptoed slyly to the Cortina and rapped with his knuckles on the glass.

'For God's sake,' shouted Patrick, and he leapt across the gravel and knocked Aldo on his back upon the grass. 'Haven't we had enough agitation for one day? Can't you see the woman's sleeping it off?'

The men murmured at Aldo's rough treatment. Patrick put his hand to his forehead and forced himself to smile. He helped Aldo to his feet and brushed him down with his large mauve hand scratched in a score of places. The workers were not rash enough to criticize him; every week he came into work with his face gashed or his mouth bruised from asserting himself outside the public house on a Saturday night. They closed ranks about the demoralized Aldo, and Patrick led the way down the road to the café with Brenda and Vittorio lagging two paces behind.

They had tea paid for by Vittorio, who seemed quite ready to put his hand in his pocket, and packets of dry little biscuits gritty with raisins. The men sprawled across the soiled tables and passed the postcard of the monkey from hand to hand. A waitress with enormous breasts wiped at the plastic cloths with a square of rag and was openly admired. She had yellow hair and a faint ginger down on her narrow lip. Freda, thought Brenda and closed her eyes, but already she could no longer visualize clearly that round face with the painted lids.

After a time Rossi left the café and wandered about outside, hands behind his back and chin sunk on his chest. Patrick nudged Brenda and indicated she should go outside and talk to him.

'No,' she protested, pursing her mouth edged with crumbs, and he pinched her quite hard on her thigh and frowned.

'Talk to him, that's all I ask.'

He wasn't as he had been in the bathroom. He was no longer shy and full of reverence. She bridled and moved her leg away and chipped a raisin from her tooth.

Vittorio was perpetually in the dark – the strange accent of the Irishman and the mumblings of Brenda confused him. He listened politely to the men discussing the placid lions, nodding in all the right places, his eyes continually flickering from Brenda to Patrick and back again. Under his fingers the picture postcard buckled at the corners. Patrick removed his cap and laid it on a ledge. Exposed, his flaring ears burned pinkly beneath his copper-coloured hair. I don't like him without his hat, thought Brenda. Come to think of it, she didn't like him at all. She actually preferred Rossi with his troublesome ways and his black and tangled curls. Excusing herself, she pushed her way from the table and went outside on to the lawn. They paced in silence for a time, up and down the path outside the window. They could hear the clatter of cups and the hiss of the coffee machine. Now and then she sensed Patrick's face at the glass, and when they reached the corner of the café building she took Rossi by the arm and marched him away to a ditch at the side of a fence and leapt clear over it into a field. He dithered on the other side and was reluctant to follow.

'Come on,' she said. 'I want to tell you something,' and he scrambled awkwardly over the cut in the ground, dipping one foot into muddy water and shaking it like a dog, one suede shoe turned black and the turn-up of his trouser soaked.

'Never mind,' she said impatiently, and she ducked down behind a hillock of damp grass and smoothed her purple cloak. 'You must know,' she said, when he had sat down beside her, fussing about his saturated shoe and sulkily wiping at it with a handkerchief, 'that what we've done is very wrong.'

He was like a child being scolded. He tossed his head at the injustice of it and refused to speak.

'Police,' she said, thinking of the night they had taken Mrs Haddon away, 'ask an awful lot of questions – all sorts of things that don't seem to have anything to do with what actually happened. They'll want to know what she said to you when you went into the bushes. Patrick's hinting something funny went on.'

He said: 'It is all happening too quick. I cannot think.' But he was once again the cellar manager whose eye was anxious, almost calculating.

'Well, you'd better. I'm warning you. Patrick thinks you hurt Freda.' She was speaking too quickly for him. 'Don't you see? He's got that cut on the eye and he had a fight with her in the church.'

'He never like Mrs Freda –'

'He threw stones at her when she was in the woods –'

'He knock Aldo to the ground. He is a violent man.'

'Yes,' she said. They were piling blame upon the Irishman, brick by brick; they sat there silently remembering.

After a while she said: 'You've got nothing to be worried about. We ought to go to the police now.'

'No.'

'It's your car she's sitting in. You've got the licence.'

'It's not my fault.'

'Well, they'll want to know why you let them put her in your car.'

He did see what she meant but he shook his head. 'No police.'

'Why on earth not?' She was getting quite irritated by him. She wanted it all settled and the landlady told and the aunt in Newcastle informed – she might even ring Stanley. 'Patrick,' she said loudly, speaking very slowly and pronouncing every word clearly, 'is trying to blame you. He says there was glass under her jumper. And I saw you go into the bushes. I'll have to tell the police. If you tell lies they always find out and it looks worse.'

'What glass is this?' he asked. 'What glass under her jumper?'

'Not under it. Stuck in the fluff in the back. And he wanted to know about your watch.'

'My watch,' he repeated in a low voice and stared blankly at the smashed timepiece on his wrist.

A long sigh escaped him. He played idly with his mud-stained handkerchief.

'It's all for the best,' she said.

Haltingly he began to tell her a story.

'When Mrs Freda came into the office and say she tell me to leave you alone, I am very angry. She mention Mr Paganotti . . .'

As he remembered the incident he flushed with renewed rage. She had been so bullying and unladylike, thumping her fist on his desk like a man. He had not known how to deal with her. When his wife had come to the factory with her niece from Casalecchio di Reno he could hardly breathe for fear Freda would march in and denounce him. When she did come, and asked him if she could use the telephone, his heart had nearly stopped beating. How could he let her use the phone with his wife sitting on her chair, listening? Hadn't he told his wife that Mr Paganotti had arranged the Outing long ago and no women were going? Freda had stood there smiling, shuffling his beautifully ordered labels on their shelves. He did not dare tell her to go away. Her pink lips had glistened; she had been so confident. And later Vittorio had seemed upset and anxious. Twice he went to the main door of the factory and looked up and down the road . . .

'But I didn't believe her. I think she just say it to upset me.'

She was always upsetting people, he thought, interfering between him and Mrs Brenda, causing everybody trouble. She had made advances to Vittorio. She had invited him round to her room and given him brandy stolen from Mr Paganotti. She wanted him to take her out to a restaurant. In the office she had whispered into Vittorio's ear as if they were betrothed . . .

'And Vittorio did not want to come on the Outing. In the street I have to persuade him. He want to go home. He say she is always arguing.'

Vittorio had made him ring the coach firm and cancel the van, so that nobody could go into the country. It was not good having to ring the man and tell him he did not want his van. He had felt ashamed doing such a thing. Vittorio had said they must go to the factory on the Sunday as if nothing happen . . . then they would all go home . . . only, when they got to the factory, it seemed a pity to waste the day, he had his sandwiches . . . besides his cousin Aldo Gamberini insist they go, and Salvatore have his car . . .

'When we play the football I think we are all having a good time. The little confusion in the fortress – pah, it is all forgotten. When we go on the horses I think Vittorio too is happy. He look at Freda as if he love her.'

It was true. Vittorio was an educated man: Mr Paganotti, his uncle, had put him through college. He had studied art – poetry. When he had looked at Mrs Freda on her horse it was as if he were reading something in one of his books. He was learning something. It was not just the wine that made him smile at her so. It had seemed a simple thing to suggest that Vittorio take her into the woods. How could he refuse? The sun was shining – the little birds were singing.

'I want us all to be happy, all to go into the woods for a little jump out. I ask Vittorio to take Freda for a walk. The men are happy playing football – the four of us – but he is angry. He say Freda will tell his uncle, Mr Paganotti, that he go to her room and try to get into the bed. I want to help my friend. I wait a little.'

The wine had made him excited. When he had walked over the grass his head was filled with pictures of Freda – alone in her room in a black gown drinking Mr Paganotti's brandy – lying on her back in the sunshine. When she rode the black horse her buttocks were like two round melons.

'I go into the bushes to ask Freda not to go to Mr Paganotti.' Rossi began to tremble. He crumpled his handkerchief into his palm.

'Go on,' said Brenda. 'What did she say?'

'I do not see her. She is talking to Vittorio.'

'She couldn't have been.' Brenda was bursting with resentments. She didn't understand why Vittorio had told lies about Freda; she didn't understand why Rossi pretended Vittorio had been in the bushes. She wanted to hit the little Italian sitting there not telling her the truth – she wanted to go home.

'Well,' she said nastily, 'it seems fishy to me. And I don't suppose the police will like it either.'

Suddenly she didn't want to wear the purple cloak any longer; it wasn't her property. She unfastened the collar and shrugged it from her shoulders. She didn't know why she was so bothered about the truth. Who was *she* to sit in judgement? It wasn't going to make any difference to Freda.

More patiently she said: 'But I did see you come out of the bushes. I didn't see Vittorio. And you were crying in the car.'

'I walk around for a few minutes. I look at you and you are like a little girl on the grass. Then I see Vittorio go away and I go into the bushes again. I am thinking she is asleep. And when I realize – '

He stopped and lowered his eyes beginning to fill with tears. She began to cry too, out of sheer tiredness, quietly, with a great deal of sniffing.

It was almost dark now. The cafeteria was closing. There were lights coming on among the trees and the distant sound of metal doors being bolted. A cart with a hose attachment moved slowly along the road toward the lion enclosure. Patrick was disturbed that she had been absent so long. They had gone to the car to look for her. The men had called her name along the hedgerow.

'I didn't hear,' she said.

He took her by the arm and stood murmuring into her ear. The men sat on a low fence and looked in the opposite direction.

'Did he say anything?'

'He said Vittorio was in the bushes before he was.'

Patrick swore.

'Will you give up now?' she said. 'Can't we go to a police station?'

They were cheating Freda out of her death. She knew that if it had been her that had been found dead under the sky, Freda would have beat her breast and shrieked her lamentation. This way, this stuffing into cars and secret consultations, was belittling to her. You'd have thought Patrick would have know how to treat the dead, being Irish – all that weeping and wailing and fluttering of candles through the night. She gave the purple cloak to Vittorio and told him to tuck it about Freda. It wasn't until she was actually sitting in the car that she realized she was dressed all in black; her woollen dress, her dark stockings, even her shoes in shadow beneath the dashboard were entirely suitable for a funeral. She would have liked to tell Rossi but she didn't want to be flippant. He was adjusting the driving mirror, twisting it this way and that – possibly he was trying to avoid the reflection of Freda's head sunk upon her breast. She tried to escape into sleep as the car wound down the path, the red mini in front of them, but she was wide-awake, her brain teeming with images: the edge of the tablecloth blowing upwards in the wind, horses racing beside the trees, the white ball leaping toward the sky. The headlamps of the Cortina caught the distempered wall of the open-air café; the metal umbrellas wavered and were gone. She thought as they began to climb the hill that she heard the sound of an elephant trumpeting down in the paddock. Patrick and Vittorio began a desultory conversation interspersed with long silences – something about the climate of Italy. They sounded as if they had just met while waiting for a train.

'In the south it is different.'

'So I've heard. I read a bit once in a paper about Naples.'

'That too is hot,' said Vittorio.

'Dirty place by all accounts,' Patrick said.

'It is a port. You know, the docks – refuse – fruit.'

'Terrible stink in the summer. Like bodies rotting.' He reddened. Even in the dark Patrick blushed like a woman, though no one could see him.

When they entered the north side of the Park, Rossi drove very slowly. The red mini was out of sight. Already it had flashed past the picnic area and was out of the Park approaching the roundabout.

The headlamps of the Cortina pierced the darkness. Brenda saw the dull gleam of the timber fence in the distance. The car crawled along the verge and stopped. Rossi switched off the engine. There was a little silvery noise as the key dangled for one instant in the ignition. They could hear one another breathing. When the wind rustled through the black grass it was like a long-drawn-out sigh.

'Well,' said Patrick, 'we got to get something settled. Between the four of us.'

Five, thought Brenda. As her eyes grew accustomed to the darkness she could make out the shape of the cut-down oak and the grey mass of the bushes beyond. They'd left a barrel of wine on the stump of the tree. If they intended to go on hiding Freda, they ought to get rid of that barrel – it was circumstantial evidence.

'It is best,' said Vittorio, 'if we tell each other the truth.' He sounded a long way off, as if he was outside somewhere, calling to them. 'For myself I have nothing to hide.' He could not however help putting his hands over his face in a

131

gesture of despair.

'Well, I have,' Patrick said. 'I've been in trouble before with the police.'

Brenda stopped herself in the nick of time from turning round. She trembled at the narrow escape and the implications of his words. She'd been alone with him in the bathroom for hours – she'd even locked the door – and she'd have gone a walk with him in the woods if he had asked her, simply to get away from Rossi.

He said: 'Nothing I'd be ashamed to tell me own mother. Fights, I mean – having a drop too much. I don't want to put meself in their hands. Before you know where you are, you've said one thing, and haven't they written it down as something else?'

Brenda wished he wouldn't talk in that ridiculous accent. Everything he said was a question. She knew the sort of trouble he meant. Stanley didn't like the police either, though God knows why: they had often brought him home when he had fallen into a ditch on the way back from the Little Legion. The Park at night reminded her of the countryside she had left: the lights of the town twinkling away to the right, the spidery branches of the trees – if she opened the window she might hear the hooting of an owl.

'Isn't it peaceful,' she murmured, though nobody heard.

On the rare occasions when she and Stanley had gone out together, walking the three miles to the village, she had always complained of a stitch in her side. More than once she had sneered at the type of entertainment offered in the Legion – the smart alec in the teddy-boy suit clutching a microphone and singing 'Delilah' at the top of his lungs. They thought her stuck-up in the Legion, even though she broadened her vowels when she spoke to them, even though she tried to play billiards. It wasn't as if she was too different from the others, there were plenty of Polish labourers left over from the war, and Pakistani immigrants who worked in the mills. She was always very polite to everyone. She never made a scene, not even when Stanley fell down the step into the Gents' and cut his forehead, but he seemed constantly uneasy in her presence. He struck her repeatedly and painfully on the thigh and told her to sup up. When they were given a lift home in a car the farmhouse sat in the valley like an orange square, tiny – his mother's window was lit by a lamp that was never extinguished, not even in sleep. The white gate at the roadside shone in the headlamps. The path down to the house was worn with rivulets of rain. Stones littered the way. Sheep floundered to their feet as Stanley ran zig-zag down the slope, urinating as he went. The whole earth swelled upwards like a vast warm bosom.

'It was my fault,' she suddenly said. She was unaware that Rossi had cried out a moment previously the name of Mr Paganotti. 'I shouldn't have been nasty to her. I shouldn't have upset her. Then she wouldn't have gone to the bushes in the first place.'

'For Christ's sake,' shouted Patrick. He leaned forward in his seat and attempted to put an arm about her shoulder in an awkward gesture of sympathy, and Freda slithered slowly downwards along the plastic seating. They got out of the car in a panic, slamming the doors and running to the tree stump as if it was a place of refuge. Rossi was moaning. He ran in a circle round and round the oak and the empty barrel of wine. All at once he darted away into the darkness. They could hear for a moment the rush of his body and the low keening he made; then he had gone. They strained their eyes trying to see into the blackness.

'Where's he gone?' whispered Patrick.

'He will come back,' said Vittorio. 'He is very highly strung. Very sensitive. He will come back.' He had a nice voice, caressing; he sounded full of compassion.

Brenda was shivering without her cloak. The men went back to the car and called her when they had propped Freda upright. She hurled herself into the front seat and curled up with her arms about her knees and pressed her chattering teeth against her wrists.

Patrick was giving up the idea of trying to make the Italians confess. They were too foreign – Vittorio clammed up like a shell and Rossi somewhere out there in the darkness blubbing like a baby. They must get back to London quick and put Freda somewhere for the night. He regretted that he had wasted so much time rushing about the countryside. In the morning he would either have thought of something or would get on the boat home and leave them to sort it out. He had a radio he could pawn, and a fellow he knew at the bar of the Waterford Castle owed him a few quid. Brenda was no use to him. She never said what she meant. She would hide him one moment if she was asked, and betray him the next.

Vittorio had a pain in his chest. His head ached. Had she been alive, Freda would have been stroking his thigh in the dark. Perhaps she was the lucky one, to go quickly and so young. For himself, years hence, there might be disease — pain: like an olive left on the ground he would wither and turn black. Gloomily he shifted his knee and imagined Freda had grown very cold: the chill of her shoulder as it pressed against him, struck him like a blow. The rim of her ear, dimly seen through the fronds of hair, burned like ice.

Now and then a car came swishing up the road; light splashed over the windows like a deluge of water and drained away instantly. After a quarter of an hour had passed Rossi came back to the car and lowered himself into the driving seat. He was breathing heavily as if he had run for miles. Vittorio said something to him and he nodded his head. When he switched on the engine, his fingers in the tiny illumination were soiled, the nails rimmed with dirt.

On the motorway the Cortina kept to the slow lane and was constantly overtaken.

'Faster,' urged Patrick, but Rossi took no heed.

Brenda hated going fast: it was dreadful having to trust her life to someone else. At any moment Rossi could lose control of the wheel and spin them all to pieces. Danger was all around her: the people hurtling along the road, the aeroplanes overhead coming in to land, sailing like railway carriages above the fragile fences – an aircraft, leaving the landing strip of the nearby airport, zoomed upward on a collision course. She kept one hand on the button of the door, ready to jump out should the car swerve or the planes begin to fall.

'Step on it,' said Patrick, like a gangster in a movie. 'We've got to dump her somewhere for the night.' And they rocked together as they drove.

Brenda was searching the outskirts of the town for resting places for Freda. She recoiled from the word 'dump' – surely he couldn't be serious? So many discoveries about him in so short a time made her tremble all over with misgivings. She saw the doorway of a church, a partially demolished house. At Shepherd's Bush a black angel flew on a plinth amidst the poplar trees. They passed the green dome of the Music Hall. They spun through the park – a dog stood frozen in the yellow wedge of the headlamps – and into the glare of the High Street. The clock outside the launderette stood at five minutes to nine as they turned the corner and drew up outside the shuttered factory.

The mini took a wrong turning just off the M1. The men were philosophical. They had the remains of the wine to sustain them.

'Such a way to behave,' said Salvatore, thinking of the wanton figure in the back of the Cortina.

'But splendid on a horse,' Gino observed grudgingly. He preferred thinner women; he was himself puny in stature, brittle in the leg and cavernous in the cheek.

Aldo seemed disconcerted that once again his cousin had disappeared. He had come to the factory in Rossi's car and dreaded lest he have to return by tube. He was fuddled by the Beaujolais and weary from his game of football. Salvatore was willing to go out of his way and take him to his door, but Aldo wouldn't hear of it.

'I came with him,' he said stubbornly. 'I will return with him.'

It seemed obvious that Rossi would take the English women to their house. Possibly she would have to be lifted in some way up the stairs. They agreed they would have a lot to tell their fellow workers when they met in the morning

– the coming and going in the fortress . . . the argument between Vittorio and Rossi . . . the rowing between the two English ladies . . . the return of the Irishman with his face torn . . . the sight of Mrs Freda being supported from the bushes . . . If only Amelio and Stefano had been there to see how it was.

There followed a time of silence while they thought of the less fortunate members of the party who had never journeyed beyond the wall of the factory.

'Surely,' said Aldo, 'they will have their money back.'

They almost missed Rossi's car parked at the side of the road. They had not thought it would be there; they expected to find it outside the house of the English girls. They stopped and walked to the alleyway. The shutter was rolled up. It was unheard of; it was unauthorized. How could Rossi be so bold as to enter Mr Paganotti's business premises after closing time? Never, except at Christmas when Mr Paganotti held a little party in his office and danced stiffly with his secretary, had they known such a thing. They stole up the alleyway and hovered outside the pass door. Gino removed his hat. Pushing the heavy door inwards, they crept down the passageway to the bottling floor. It was dark save for a single yellow bulb burning beneath the roof. The plant stood silent under its ragged cover; a rat rustled beneath the cardboard boxes. Mrs Brenda was slumped on a crate by the wall. Vittorio and Rossi, heaving and straining, were pushing Mrs Freda, stretched out upon a trolley, into the mouth of the lift.

They ran in their best clothes, slapping the concrete floor with their damp shoes. They bent over the sprawled figure, shoulder to shoulder.

'Don't look,' began Vittorio.

'*Madre dì Dio,*' cried out Aldo Gamberini, rocking and wailing, already in his black.

Brenda had scurried home along the familiar street. The scene in the factory, the weeping of the men, the wild exclamations of Rossi and Vittorio – all restraint gone now they were not alone in their predicament – had embarrassed her. She found it difficult not to smile. She turned her face to the wall and bared her teeth. When Rossi and Vittorio took Freda up to the first floor, the men ceased their lamentations. They turned their faces to the ceiling and listened to the rumble of the trolley across the boards. After an interval the lift descended. The men lined up inside, jostling for space, each with a hat held to his breast – they were like a family posing for a photograph. The dim bulb raked their oiled hair with auburn light. Creaking, the lift ascended – a line of shoes, caked with mud, merged into the darkness.

She waited a few minutes but nobody came down. Freda's sheepskin coat, mingled with the purple cloak, lay abandoned on the dusty floor.

She decided they had forgotten her.

When she entered the bed-sitting room she saw the table set for two, the saucer of olives, the silver slab of the butter. The sight of the folded napkins beneath the blue-rimmed plates affected her far more than the lilac scarf trailing the edge of the funeral trolley. She could not bear to lie down on the bed. She dared not approach the chair at the side of the grate – the worn cushion bore the imprint of Freda's weight. There was nothing of herself in the room: everywhere she saw Freda – the magazine beside the window, the lacy brassière dangling above the gasfire, pinned to the marble top of the mantelshelf by the ticking clock. She wilted under the continued presence of Freda. She would rather have stayed in the car, the factory. She had not realized how like a garden of remembrance the room would be. If she listened, all she could hear was the ticking of the clock and the minute crackling of the dried leaves on the dreadful table spread for a romantic supper. After a moment, trapped in the centre of the carpet, she heard a tap on the window. Someone was throwing gravel at the glass. She laid her cheek to the pane and peered down into the street. It was Patrick.

Rigidly he stared up at her, his legs tapering to a point on the paving stones. She ran to the landing wild with relief at not being on her own, and stopped. Freda had called her a victim, had said she was bent on destroying herself – it was possible Patrick had returned because she knew too much. When they had carried Freda into the factory the Irishman had supervised, held open the door, fumbled for the light switch. By the time they had laid her on the trolley he had gone.

She stroked the banister rail. She remembered Patrick in the bathroom winding the length of string tightly about the hook in the ceiling. She clapped her hands to her cheeks and her mouth flew open. She must at all costs preserve herself. She went back into the room and struggled to lift up the window. Propping the tennis racket into place, she crawled out on to the balcony.

'What do you want?' she called. She saw he was holding a bottle of wine.

'Let me in.'

'I can't.'

'Let me in.'

'The landlady won't let us have people in after midnight.'

'For God's sake, it's only after ten.'

She couldn't believe it. She thought it was the middle of the night – they had got up so early, the day had gone on and on.

'I'm tired.'

He made to climb the steps. He lifted his hand to pound the brass knocker.

'Wait,' she called in desperation, fearful the two nurses would let him in. 'I'll come down.' If he attacked her on the step she would scream or run toward a passing car.

'What did they do with her?' he asked, when she had opened the door.

'They've put her upstairs among the furniture.'

'Let me in. I'm parched for a cup of tea.'

'I can't.' She sat down on the step and shivered.

'I pinched a bottle of wine. Do you not want a drop of wine?'

'I'd be sick,' she said.

He put the bottle on the step beside a withered wallflower. He removed his cap and sat down. He looked like a grocer's boy – he ought to be riding a bicycle, she thought, delivering butter and eggs, and whistling.

'What will they say?' she moaned. 'Whatever will happen?'

He tried to smile at her but his mouth quivered.

'I don't know what to do,' he admitted. 'I'm wore out.'

'It's awful up there,' she told him. 'Her things – her clothes – everywhere.'

'I'm wore out,' he repeated sullenly, as if she had no right to burden him. A door opened in the flats opposite. An old lady leaned over her balcony and called quaveringly: 'Tommy! Tommy! I've got your dinner, Tommy.'

'Upstairs,' said Brenda, 'the table's laid.'

'I'm not hungry.'

'No. I mean for her and Vittorio.'

'Not for you?'

'No,' she said. 'Just for them.'

The leaves of the privet hedge fragmented in the light of the street lamp. Shadows shifted across his face. He drew a handkerchief from the pocket of his mackintosh and laid it between them on the step. He unfolded it. There were a few pieces of glass.

She said: 'That's Rossi's hankie.'

'I know. The glass is from his broken watch. They were in the bushes.'

'What did you bring them back for?'

'I didn't,' he said. 'Rossi did. When we stopped on the way home didn't he go off into the night? I pinched it from his jacket when we went into the factory.'

'Oh,' she said, 'you *are* clever' – not quite sincerely. She didn't know what to think and was having difficulty in concentrating. Even if she wanted to stay on in the bed-sitting room, could she afford it? Could her father be persuaded to send her a little more money? When people found out about Freda it was bound to get into the papers and her mother would tell her father not to send her any money at all, just to force her to come home.

They'd go out shopping, and her mother would tell her to stay in the car so the neighbours wouldn't see. She'd tell her what clothes to wear, throw out her black stockings and buy her a pink hat from the Bon Marché. They'd put her in a deck chair in the garden and treat her like an invalid, only sternly. She'd never be allowed to stay in bed in the morning, not after the first week. Now that my moment has come, she thought, my chosen solitude, can I stand the expense?

'I'm going in,' she said. 'I'm dropping.'

He twisted his cap in his hands round and round between his drawn-up knees.

'Suit yourself.' He plopped the handkerchief with its glass fragments into her unwilling hands. 'I'll leave this with you.'

She held the handkerchief at some distance from her as if it was in danger of exploding. She didn't protest, because she was so glad he didn't insist on following her into the house.

'Good night,' she murmured.

When he said goodbye she couldn't hear for the slam of the door. She took a pillow and blankets from the bed and went upstairs to the bathroom. If anybody tried to use the toilet in the night it was just too bad. Freda said the man upstairs was a dirty bugger anyway – he probably peed in the sink. The busybodies on the ground floor were hopefully on night duty. Before she bolted the door she remembered the open window.

When she crossed the room she put an olive in her mouth, but it tasted bitter and she laid it down again on the cloth. Freda's brassière trembled in the draught.

CHAPTER EIGHT

Maria was told by her brother-in-law Anselmo. Appalling contortions distorted her face. He clapped his hand over her mouth, for fear she screeched like a railway train, and lowered her into Rossi's chair behind the desk. Though normally she would have leapt upright out of respect for the manager's office, she now remained slumped in her seat, eyes rolling above his bunched fingers. It was a blessing Vittorio had a small glass of brandy ready for when she was more composed – under the circumstances she drained it at one gulp. She flapped her pinny to cool her cheeks and waited while Vittorio fetched Brenda from the washroom, where she had been more or less all morning retching over the basin. The two women embraced and drew apart sniffing.

'It's God's work,' wailed Maria.

'Yes,' said Brenda, although she couldn't be sure. She felt really poorly: her stomach was upset. She was tired out from her night in the bathroom, vivid with dreams.

'We must prepare her. We must see to her.' Maria had laid out an aunt and an infant son of Anselmo's but never in such conditions.

'I can't do anything,' cried Brenda in alarm. 'I'm not going up there.'

Outside the window the men were grouped thinly about the bottling plant. Throughout the morning they had gone in pairs into the ancient lift and visited Freda, returning with calm faces and eyes glittering with excitement. They whispered frantically. The machine rattled and circled. They looked up at the Virgin on the wall and crossed themselves. Rossi had been called into the main office by Mr Paganotti an hour previously and had not returned.

'I have to have water and clean cloths,' said the dedicated Maria, ' – clean garments to lie in.' It was inconceivable that they should use the sponges on the bench.

'I could go home and get her flannel,' offered Brenda, 'and her black nightie.'

Maria wouldn't hear of the black nightie – there must be nothing dark – but she accepted the flannel and asked her to bring a bowl and powder and a hairbrush. It seemed silly to Brenda, such a fuss twenty-four hours too late: Freda wasn't going anywhere.

The telephone rang, and Anselmo said Mr Paganotti wanted to speak to Vittorio. They all went very quiet, thinking of Rossi and the state he was in. Perhaps he had broken down in the main office and told Mr Paganotti that there was a body upstairs among his relatives' tables and chairs. Vittorio nodded his head several times. He stood very straight, inclining his head deferentially as if Mr Paganotti were actually in the room.

'Go, go,' said Maria, shooing Brenda with her pinny toward the door. 'Fetch the cloth.' To fortify her for the task ahead she allowed herself a little more brandy.

As Brenda opened the front door the nurse from the downstairs room came out into the hall in a dressing-gown and slippers. 'Oh, it's you,' she said. 'Aren't you working?'

'I've just popped back,' Brenda said.

The nurse let her climb a few stairs before she called: 'Is your friend in?'

Brenda clung to the banister rail and stopped. 'She's out just now.'

'Well, will you tell her I'd like my serviettes back. I lent them to her yesterday. She said she only wanted them for one evening.'

'Serviettes?' said Brenda, her heart pounding.

'I want to take them in when I go on duty. I can have them laundered for nothing.'

Brenda looked down at her. She had an almost transparent skin and dark eyes that were used to detecting signs of rising temperature and internal disorder.

'Actually,' said Brenda, 'she went away last night – abroad.'

Freda had been saving for years to go on the Continent. She had never gone because she had never saved, she had a post-office book that she put part of her wages in every month and drew them out the next.

'Lucky her,' said the nurse dangling her hospital towel. 'I expect she could do with a break after her mother dying like that.'

It was simple to explain really, once she got started. There was a bit of money due from Freda's mother's estate, not much but enough for a holiday: and her Uncle Arthur who was in a good way of doing had advanced her funds so that she could get away. She'd always wanted to go to Spain – she was very interested in flamenco dancing – so she just went off all of a sudden. Made up her mind, packed her bag, and went.

'How long for?' asked the nurse, scraping an envious cheek with the handle of her toothbrush. Brenda said it depended on the weather. It was winter after all – it wasn't as if she was going to lie on some beach. She might come back next week or she might never.

'Never?' cried the nurse.

Brenda was laughing. 'You know what I mean. She might, she might not.' She continued up the stairs shaking with laughter. 'Who knows,' she called from the bend of the stairs and she stumbled upwards squealing and gasping for breath.

When Brenda returned with the pastel-coloured toilet bag and the washing-up bowl, the workers were crowded into the concrete bunker under the fire escape. She could hear them shouting as she went up the alleyway toward the pass door. The bottling plant stood idle. Alone, old Luigi, undeterred by the drama, was labelling with ferocious speed. Stefano was on guard beside the lift.

'You go,' he said pointing his finger straight up in the air. She said, No, she wouldn't thank you, she'd just brought a few things for Maria.

He told her to fetch Salvatore from the bunker to keep watch while he took the bowl upstairs.

The men, wrapped in pieces of old carpeting, were sitting on upturned boxes, rolling cigarettes and gesticulating.

She felt terribly out of it. The way they carried on, so engrossed, faces drawn with grief, eyes mournfully gazing at their unwrapped luncheons – you'd have thought Freda was a relative. She wondered what Rossi had told them. Surely he hadn't said Patrick had broken her neck – nobody could be certain. Rossi seemed terribly agitated. He was trembling and arguing with Vittorio.

'What's wrong now?' she asked.

Vittorio said: 'Mr Paganotti wants the first floor to be cleared of the furniture. He is going up in the lift this very afternoon to take the look around.'

'Well, she can't stay there anyway,' began Brenda, 'she'll start – ' But she couldn't continue. She wasn't sure how quickly bodies began to smell – perhaps here in the factory, with the temperature close to freezing, Freda could be preserved for ever. 'What's he want to shift the furniture for now?' she asked. 'What's the sudden hurry?'

'Mr Paganotti call me in,' cried Rossi. 'His secretary is sitting there, she is smiling and asking me how the Outing go. Did we have the nice time in the country?'

'How awkward,' said Brenda. Mr Paganotti's secretary came from a well-to-do family in Rome. Nobody had liked to ask her on the Outing. She could hardly be classed a worker.

'I look at the floor,' continued Rossi. 'Mr Paganotti ask me if I like the Stately Home. If it had been an interesting Stately Home.'

That was kind of him, thought Brenda. Fancy Mr Paganotti remembering a thing like that.

'Mr Paganotti say he is re-organizing his business premises. He is going to get the new machinery, expand – he need more office space. For the ordering, the accountancy. He want the furniture gone from the first floor.'

'I would have died,' breathed Brenda, feeling terribly sorry for Rossi.

Mr Paganotti, it appeared, had noticed how disturbed

Rossi had been. He had frowned. He had dug his thumb into the pocket of his beautiful striped waistcoat. He had asked what was wrong.

'I tell him,' said Rossi, 'that the men are very busy at the moment. I say there is the sherry consignment from Santander – the barrels have to be emptied and ready for return shipment tomorrow. I tell him that if the barrels are not ready for return there is a storage charge.' Rossi spread out his hands, palm upwards, to show he had concealed nothing. 'Mr Paganotti understand at once. He say it is a pity but it cannot be helped. He tell me to get on with my work and he himself will go upstairs later in the afternoon and look around.'

'You could tell him the lift was broken,' said Brenda. 'Or not safe.'

'It has never been safe,' Vittorio said. 'But then he go up the stairway.'

'Not if you pile the stairs with furniture, blocking the way.'

'Ah,' cried Rossi. 'That is it.' And the men, when it had been explained to them, thumped the table enthusiastically and scrambled out of the concrete bunker to begin the barricade at once.

'What did you say to the men?' asked Brenda, left alone with Vittorio.

'I say nothing.'

'Did you say Patrick did it?'

'I say nothing. I merely say there has been an accident. I say it will look bad for Rossi and for me. We are not English. The Irishman has a grudge against us. They understand. They do not want our families to be shamed, our children – they do want to bring shame to the good name of my uncle Mr Paganotti.'

'Didn't they think it was a bit funny?'

'Funny?'

Brenda thought he was incredible; they were all unbelievable. In their loyalty to each other, united in a foreign country, Freda seemed to have been forgotten. She said sharply: 'The girl in my house just asked me for her serviettes back.' He looked at her without understanding. 'For your supper.'

'What supper?'

'Freda was hoping you'd come home with her. She'd bought butter and stuff. And she borrowed things to wipe your mouth on.'

'I do not know about any supper,' he said.

'Well, she thought you might come back. I told the nurse she'd gone abroad.'

'Abroad,' he repeated.

'To Spain. I said she liked dancing.' And again she burst into little trills of laughter, her face quite transformed by smiles.'

'You are overwrought,' he said, and he poured her some wine from the jug on the table. While she was still laughing, stuffing her fingers into her cheeks and showing all her teeth, a thought struck him. He began to tremble with excitement. He ran from the bunker and went to find Rossi. Brenda fell asleep with her face on the table amidst a pile of sandwiches.

When Brenda woke from a dream, she didn't feel ill any more or cross. She had been in a cinema with Freda: Freda was wearing a trouser suit and one of those floppy hats with some cloth flowers on the brim. She complained bitterly that she couldn't see the bloody screen. The men in the row behind said 'Sssh!' loudly and kicked the back of the seat. Brenda whispered she should take her hat off. 'Why should I?' said Freda; and Brenda remembered a little doggerel her mother had taught her, something about a little woman with a great big hat . . . went to the pictures and there she sat. Freda shrieked and recited rapidly . . . man behind couldn't see a bit . . . finally got tired of it. Somehow it made Brenda very happy that Freda too knew the little rhyme. She beamed in the darkness. She turned and kissed Freda on the cheek and woke instantly.

Gone was the worry and the fear, the underlying resentment. Freda would have been the first to agree, it didn't matter how she had died – it wasn't any use getting all worked up about it now. Life was full of red tape, rules and formalities, papers to be signed. Hadn't Freda always been the first to decry the regimentation of the masses? If Rossi and Vittorio, still alive in a puny world, fought to protect the honour of their families, did it really matter very much? No amount of questions or criminal procedure or punishment would bring her back. Brenda was almost prepared to go up in the lift and see Freda all nice and clean from the ministrations of Maria.

She wandered into the alleyway and through the pass door to the factory. Aldo Gamberini and Stefano, doing the work that eight men had done before, were running giddily after the rotating bottles on the machine. The labelling bench, save for old Luigi, was deserted. She went into the office to find Rossi fiddling about with litmus paper and glass tubes.

'I'm all right now,' she said. 'I don't mind whose fault it was. I'll give you your handkerchief back if you like.'

'My handkerchief –' and he clapped his hand to the pocket of his overall, forgetting that he had worn his best trousers and a jumper on the Outing.

'It doesn't matter,' said Brenda, and was only slightly shocked to see the purple cloak and the sheepskin coat hanging on the back of the door. 'Have you blocked the stairs?' she asked. 'Have you stopped Mr Paganotti?'

'He has gone out,' said Rossi. 'I think he has not remembered.'

'What are you going to do tomorrow, then? He won't be out every day.'

'It was you,' he said, rising from his desk in admiration. 'You have given us the way.'

'Me? What did I do?'

'You tell us about Spain. You give us the idea.' And he paced about the office, face illuminated with appreciation. 'We will put her in a barrel – in a hogshead. It is simple. Gino is even now sawing the lid off for her entrance.'

'You're not going to put Freda in a barrel?'

'Listen,' he said. 'We now bottle the sherry. We take the sherry from the hogshead. When the barrels are empty the man come and we load the empty barrels on to the lorry. They go to the docks, back to Santander.'

'With Freda?'

'Why yes,' he said. 'It is finished.'

She looked at him. Smudges of fatigue showed under her sceptical eyes. 'And what happens when they open the barrels at the other end? Or take out the bung or whatever it's called – at Santander?' It was a lovely name; there were bound to be flamenco dancers.

'We mark the barrel as no good – bad for the wine – tainted – it is leaking. They throw it in the sea.'

'In the sea? Are you sure?'

'But yes. I have seen it when I am training. I know about these things – the unworthy barrels go in the sea.'

She didn't like to mention it, but she felt she must. 'Rossi,' she said, 'what if there's a strike at the docks? There's always some kind of a strike going on somewhere.'

He stared at her. 'What for you worry about a strike?'

'Well, she might begin to – to smell!' His mouth fell open. 'You ought to put something in the barrel with her – like brandy. To preserve her.' She couldn't look at him. She gazed at the floor.

'But we cannot use Mr Paganotti's brandy – it is very expensive – very good.'

Still, he was beginning to see what she meant. Perhaps just a little brandy. The lid would have to be clamped down very securely, so as to avoid leakage. The English girl was right. There was bound to be some kind of a strike.

'We do it,' he said. 'We put a little brandy in the barrel – just a little.'

'Well, that's very satisfactory,' Brenda said and wondered who was going to tell the aunt in Newcastle that Freda had fled to Spain.

Maria wanted flowers for Freda; she said it was no good without flowers. She came out of the lift all heated from her work, the sleeves of her frock pushed up to her elbows, her pinny streaked with damp. Vittorio said he would donate money and some should be bought from the shop on the High Street.

'Lots of flowers,' reiterated Maria, and she held her arms out to a certain width and rolled her eyes.

Brenda thought it would cost a fortune.

Rossi said in alarm: 'No, we cannot go to the High Street shop. What for are we buying flowers? Mr Paganotti might see – Mr Cavaloni the accountant – the secretary from Rome.'

Maria drooped in disappointment. Never had she laid out anyone without flowers.

After some moments it occurred to Rossi that when his wife bought washing powder earlier in the week she had returned with a plastic rose. 'A free offer,' he said excitedly.

'The washing powder isn't free,' said Brenda.

He waved his hands impatiently. 'We all buy the powder – we all go one by one and purchase the powder with the little rose.'

Throughout the afternoon the men went to the supermarket and returned with packets of powder and the free offer. Brenda paid for her packet with her own money. She felt it was a gesture. She was scandalized that the little rose turned out to be a sort of tulip on a long yellow stem.

The boyfriend of Mr Paganotti's secretary from Rome came at six o'clock in his red sports car and tooted his horn. Mr Paganotti's secretary ran out on the dot in her caramel brown coat of fur and whisked herself into the seat beside him. Five minutes later the accountant, Mr Cavaloni, escorted Mr Paganotti to his grey Bentley and held open the door with respectfully bowed head. They shook hands. A child holding a ball scraped the gleaming paintwork with his nail and was admonished. When the grey Bentley had turned the corner, Mr Cavaloni scrambled into his Ford and drove off down the street.

The workers went to the lift and rode in groups up to the first floor. Brenda had been sent by Vittorio to the Italian confectioner's in Lucas Street. She had bought dry little buns seamed with chocolate and a cake, *torta di riso*, that Maria said was a speciality of Bologna. They had cleared a dining-room table, riddled like a colander with woodworm, and laid out the cakes and a row of paper cups. Rossi had sent up five bottles of Spumanti. Before coming to pay their last respects, the men had removed their overalls and washed their hands in the yard. The hogshead of sherry, empty and with its lid neatly sawn off, stood ready by the lift. At the far end of the room, candles burning at her head and her feet, lay Freda on a couch strewn with plastic tulips. Her eyes had been closed. She wore a long white gown reaching to her ankles. Maria had removed the hand-made boots and after some thought encased her feet in a pair of tennis socks somewhat worn at the soles. Her hair, brushed and lightly curled, quivered on the grey upholstery.

'Wherever did you get that?' asked Brenda when she had first clapped eyes on the white dress. It was a nightgown, extremely old in design; fragile lace clung to the collar and cuffs.

'In Mr Paganotti's box,' explained Maria, hastening to add that it was clean and aired. She herself had heated an old steam iron found in the basement and pressed it. Thoughtfully arranged, the brown spots of damp no longer showed.

The men shyly poured out the Spumanti. Glasses had been found in the outer office. 'Careful, careful,' urged Rossi, fearful there might be breakages. They huddled at the mouth of the lift amid a pile of kitchen chairs and bric-a-brac, watching the leaping candles at the far end of the room. Brenda still wore her black dress and her stockings and the old coat that Freda had despised.

The men who had not been on the unforgettable Outing revelled in the unaccustomed festivity of the moment. The rest, worn out from the previous day and hours spent emptying the consignment of sherry at breakneck speed, rubbed their creased foreheads, and stifled yawns. Maria sat in an armchair heavy with dust; her legs did not reach the floor. Grey hair, escaping from the bunch on her neck, spilled down her back, as she rocked back and forth gulping her champagne. She remembered other places, other deaths. Her lips moved.

'Ah well,' sighed Rossi. 'It cannot be helped. It is life.'

'Aye, aye,' agreed the men, though life it was not.

Brenda gazed at the distant sofa. At this angle nothing of Freda was visible save for one big toe warm in its tennis sock and a fringe of golden curls tipping the shadowy upholstery. She remembered that Rossi had brought her here two weeks ago. He had chased her round the tables and the chairs. She had jumped over the back of the sofa and stumbled. He had leapt upon her. Down came his little red mouth in a jangle of springs and a flurry of dust. He had tried to unbutton her coat. Squealing, she rolled to the floor and fluttered her rubber gloves in his face. Freda, when told, had been scornful. 'You must be mad,' she had said. 'You wouldn't catch me lying down on that dirty old couch.' Brenda glanced at Rossi to see if he too remembered, but he was examining the barrel at the lift.

'She looks beautiful, yes?' asked Maria.

'Beautiful,' agreed Brenda. Where were Freda's clothes – her purple jumper – her knickers? I could never do anything like that, she thought, looking at Maria, not even if I was paid.

'On her splendid legs,' whispered Maria, 'there are bruises.'

'Bruises?' said Brenda.

'And on her stomach. There are bruises.'

'Oh,' said Brenda, and wondered if the ride on the horse had caused the bruises on her legs. Freda had said she was aching; she had said her thighs hurt – she hadn't mentioned her stomach.

The men were beginning to drift about the room, relaxed by the Spumanti. They opened drawers and looked inside the suitcases and found sheets of music. Gino, exhausted from his labours with a blunt saw, lay down upon a mildewed mattress and went to sleep. He sprawled with his mouth open and groaned softly.

'He is tired,' said Rossi apologetically, fearing it might

seem disrespectful. Under cover of the gloom, he put his hand on Brenda's waist and dug at her with his fingers. He drew her to a bookcase standing against the wall and pointed at the shelves.

'I think it is very good, yes? It is very valuable.' He was licking the tip of her prominent nose.

'No,' she said, 'it's mostly plywood. Look at the cheap varnish on it.'

He was offended. Nothing remotely connected with Mr Paganotti could be cheap or tawdry. Still, he did not let go of her waist.

There was quite a hum of conversation growing. The little buns crumbled to the floor. The bottles of wine emptied. The men filled their cheeks with rice cake and munched and munched. Maria, bolt upright on her chair, fingers closed and pointed at her breast, shut her eyes and prayed. Anselmo found an old gramophone with a handle; a voice reedy with age began to warble a ballad.

'*Santa Vergine*,' cried Maria out loud, and the record was abruptly removed. The turntable continued to spin round and round, slower and slower. From below came the sound of heavy banging. Someone was hitting the shutters of the loading bay with a brick. A voice, dulled at this distance, but dreadfully loud outside in the street, demanded admittance. Vittorio crossed himself. He looked about for Rossi but could not see him. The banging began again, louder this time.

'The Irishman,' whispered Aldo Gamberini, face pressed to the windows above the street.

'Let him in,' cried Vittorio. 'He will wake the town.'

Nobody moved. Like a drowning man, Vittorio ran to the lift and sank below the floor.

When he returned with Patrick they were still in their places: Maria in the chair, the men about the table, Gino asleep on the dusty mattress.

Patrick stared at the remains of the cake, the empty bottles, the flickering candles. 'For the love of God,' he said. 'What are you doing?'

The cut on his eye was already healing; in the dim light it was no longer noticeable. He saw the sofa, the hair tumbled on the padded arm, the white mound strewn with stiff and everlasting flowers.

'Where is she?' he demanded, turning on them grouped together for safety. 'Where's Brenda?'

They too looked about at the shadows, at the dull gleam of the cheap bookcase, the black cave behind a mound of boxes.

He ran to the wall. He clambered over chairs. He kicked the boxes to the ground. Clothing spilled to the floor, old books; there was the smash of disintegrating plates. But he had Rossi by the throat, lifting him bodily from the darkness by the front of his jacket, shaking him like a rattle. It seemed to the men that he would shake the breath out of his body. They hurled themselves upon Patrick. They clawed his hair. They pulled him backwards from the gasping Rossi. Brenda, dishevelled, her coat unbuttoned, treading a carpet of broken crockery, stumbled into the light. She peered short-sightedly at the ring of men. She was dreadfully alarmed and confused.

'You –' she said, 'I thought you'd gone away.'

'At a time like this?' shouted Patrick, outraged. He appeared simpler than before, his cap knocked from his head, a button torn from his mackintosh. Maria gave a small dry titter and clapped a hand over her mouth. The men, shrinking from the heavy blows they had delivered, trembled in the candlelight. Rossi straightened himself, he tugged his shirt into place, he adjusted his ruined tie.

'You have no right,' he said. 'You have not the right to touch me.' And his face crumpled at the unfairness of it.

The workers did not know what to think. If anything, they were inclined to be sympathetic to the Irishman; he was so openly broken-hearted at finding Mrs Brenda in the arms of Rossi. They brushed Patrick's raincoat with tentative hands. They picked his cap from the floor and avoided Rossi's eyes.

'Have you gone mad?' choked Patrick, speaking to Brenda alone.

'I'm sorry,' she said, 'really I'm sorry. It's not what you think.'

She would have comforted him if she had known how. It was embarrassing the way he was looking at her in front of everybody.

Vittorio was shouting at Rossi. Rossi had stepped back a pace and was blinking watery eyes.

'How could you?' said Patrick again, as if she had fallen from a pedestal.

'We were only looking at the bookcase,' she whined. 'You know what Rossi's like, I told you before –' and stopped because she never had – it was Freda she had told.

He sat down on the mattress beside Gino as if he was tired.

'You're never going to bury her up here,' he said, jerking his head at the funeral couch.

'We've thought of a plan,' she said. 'It's quite a good one.' It didn't seem fair to let him go on suffering, worrying that he was going to be found out – waiting for the knock on the door, the uniformed men on the step. 'Nothing can go wrong. You don't have to be frightened.'

'I didn't do it,' he said. 'For God's sake, I never did it.' He jabbed a finger in the direction of Rossi. 'That bastard did it I tell you. I never touched a hair of her head.'

'Oh well,' she murmured, 'it doesn't matter.' Appalled, she saw that tears were squeezing out his hurt blue eyes. She sank down on the mattress beside him and would have liked to put an arm about his shoulder.

Vittorio came to her and whispered: 'We are going to put her in the barrel. It's getting late.'

'I'm going,' she said, starting up in horror. 'I can't watch that.'

'Go downstairs to the office,' he said, 'with the Irishman. There is something to tell you.' And he put a hand under Patrick's elbow and helped him to his feet. 'Go and wait,' he said.

Brenda took Patrick to the lift. He shuffled his feet like an old man, all the fight gone out of him They waited for some time, Patrick slumped behind Rossi's desk, herself standing looking out of the window at the factory floor and the stacked cartons.

'They're very kind really,' she said. 'They're nice men.'

'What are they doing with her now?' he asked.

'Doing things – putting her in a container.'

'A container?'

'In a barrel,' she said, 'with brandy. They're exporting her.'

She thought he might laugh, but he didn't. She herself bit her lip in case.

'Is it done?' she asked, when Vittorio and Rossi came into the office. She wondered if they had stuffed the plastic tulips in as well.

'No,' said Vittorio, 'the men are working now.' He looked at Rossi and at the Irishman behind the desk. He said something in Italian.

'I want to tell you what happened,' said Rossi. 'It is I.'

The Irishman did not appear to be listening.

'He is wanting to tell you the truth,' said Vittorio.

'Whose idea was it to put her in a barrel?' asked Patrick.

Rossi threw up his hands in despair. He prowled about the office. Catching sight of his reflection in the mirror beside the door he took a comb from his pocket and attended to his hair.

'Tell him,' urged Vittorio.

'It is I,' cried Rossi, turning from the mirror and steeling himself to go quite near the Irishman. He put his hands on the desk and lowered his head. 'I do it.'

'What happens at the other end when they try to fill the barrels up again? Or this end, if old Paganotti mistakes the barrel and siphons himself a drink? By Jesus, there'd be more body in the brandy than he bargained for.' He giggled nervously.

Vittorio said slowly: 'Rossi is wanting to tell you what happened to Mrs Freda.' In his desperation he hit the blotter with his fist and the glass tubes rolled together and jingled. The Irishman concentrated on Rossi.

'It is very bad,' began Rossi, 'but it is the truth.' He

looked briefly at Vittorio who nodded encouragingly. 'I swear it.' He brought his hands passionately to his breast. 'I am at the fence watching everyone play football. I see Mrs Freda go into the bushes. I see Vittorio go into the bushes. When Vittorio go out I go back in again.' He flapped his wrist back and forth indicating the to-and-fro among the bushes. 'She is hot and she is pushing her jumpers from her stomach.'

He was standing now with his feet wide apart, bracing himself for some shock or blow about to be administered. Curiously they watched as he rolled his jersey above the waistband of his trousers. There was a button missing, a glimpse of vest.

'I am a man,' he said. 'I am drinking. I see her skin as she breathe in and out with the hotness, the little bits wobbling. I make to put my arms round her but she is too tall. I only reach her here.' He was miming the incident now. He leaned forward from the waist and circled the air with his arms. His curls bounced upon his brow. 'She say to me – she say – ' Evidently it was too painful for him to repeat.

Vittorio frowned and tapped the desk lightly with his finger tips.

Rossi continued: 'She take one little step backwards like so. She falls away from me. Her neck goes like this – ' He was staggering in a ridiculous fashion away from them, jumper ruched about his chest; he was raising an arm in the air. Suddenly he reached up and yanked his head violently backwards by the hair. His mouth fell open; his tongue flickered horribly; he made a small clicking noise. He straightened, and sneaked a glance at his audience, who were sitting bolt upright watching him. Vittorio was white-faced and dismal. His brown eyes seemed to have grown larger as if to be ready for all the things he still had to see, feel. His fingers, playing with the edge of his collar, brushed his throat. Rossi pointed at the dusty floor of the office. 'She fall down. Bang. I am falling on top of her.' He landed absurdly on his knees in front of them, scrambling on all fours before the desk. 'My head bump in her stomach.' And he jerked his chin upward as if heading a ball. His eyes closed as he butted the warm swell of Freda's belly.

There was a long pause. Nobody said anything. After a moment Rossi remarked: 'There is a stone under my wrist. When I get up, my watch is no good. It is done for.'

He fell silent. He got to his feet and, red-faced, brushed the dust from his knees. Again he looked at Vittorio.

'I have forgotten nothing,' he muttered, 'nothing.' He took out the comb and raked his hair once more with a tragic expression.

It sounds reasonable, thought Brenda. She had wanted to know the exact details. It was the sort of thing that could happen to anyone, if they were tall and they were grabbed in the bushes by a small man. It certainly wasn't anything you could hang someone for.

'Well,' said Patrick grudgingly, 'just as long we know.' He sounded as if he had been cheated out of something.

Outside the office window Brenda saw Salvatore and Aldo Gamberini rolling an enormous barrel out of the lift.

Brenda wanted Patrick to come home with her and have a cup of tea: the butter and olives were still on the table. He wouldn't. He wouldn't even walk up the street with her. He strode off without a word and turned the corner. Maria said her sister was waiting. She had cried so much in the washroom when the men were battering down the barrel that her face was lop-sided. She had leant against the wall holding Freda's flannel to her eyes and moaned.

'Stop it,' Brenda had advised. 'You will make yourself ill.'

The men had swept up the crumbs and blown out the candles. Trembling at the waste they had pumped a quantity of brandy up from the basement. They had glued the lid of the barrel into place and driven nails. They had marked it as unworthy.

Vittorio jumped into the Cortina with Rossi and an unsteady Aldo Gamberini. The green shutter was rolled down in the alleyway. Anselmo adjusted the padlock and went to the car to give Rossi the key. Those who were going in the opposite direction shook hands. 'Ciao,' they murmured, clutching their briefcases and their carrier bags.

Brenda didn't want to seem pathetic, so she gave a little cheery wave and walked off under the street lamps.

She was very lonely, she would have done anything rather than walk up the darkening street alone. She couldn't eat anything, she couldn't settle in the bed-sitting room. The clock had stopped above the hanging brassière, a mouse had nibbled the corner of the butter. She remembered the rest of the doggerel that Freda had known:

Turned to woman, sitting there,
See that mouse beneath that chair,
Little woman, great big hat,
Couldn't stand the thought of that.
Up she got and left the house
Man made happy, saw no mouse.

'Ah,' she said out loud, 'what a cunning man.' She slid the folded serviettes from beneath the blue plates and went downstairs to knock at the nurse's door. Nobody answered. She shook a finger in the dark and sat down on the stairs. Her neck was terribly stiff. She rubbed at it under her hair and screwed up her eyes – and saw Freda falling backwards. Now then, she told herself, just stop it. There was no one to talk with: even the cat had been let in, safe downstairs on the landlady's hearth rug. She was like one of those old ladies in the flats, roaming the balconies for someone to call to. Resolutely she started up the stairs with the serviettes in her hand to clear the awful table. Things should be put in their place. When she went into the room the lampshade with the fringing spun round: Freda was falling – falling. Oh God, she thought, will I always see her like that? She tried to think of her running after the ball, riding the horse. She saw instead Freda trailing her coat across the grass toward the bushes. She saw Vittorio shouting at Rossi against the timber fence. She saw him take something from Rossi's wrist. He shook it; he held it to his ear. She saw Rossi coming out of the bushes. She felt the grass prickling her cheek. Vittorio was running up to Rossi; he was trying to thrust something into his hand. Rossi was standing like a man in a dream, dazed. Vittorio was buckling a watch about Rossi's wrist. Freda was falling backwards. 'I have forgotten nothing,' muttered Rossi looking at Vittorio, 'nothing.' She shook her head and wished she could stop thinking about it. Rossi was such a loyal little man. He would do anything to protect the name of Paganotti. It doesn't matter, she thought, it is no longer of the slightest importance.

She took money out of her purse and went downstairs to ring Stanley. The code number was very long: the telegraph wires ran right across the country, through Ramsbottom and down the slope to the farmhouse.

Mrs Haddon answered the phone. 'Hallo.'

'Hallo,' said Brenda. 'It's me, Brenda. Can I speak to Stanley please?'

'Mr Haddon is out at present. Would you care to leave a message?'

'I want to come home,' said Brenda at last.

'I'm afraid it's not convenient. Mr Haddon has made other arrangements. A woman from the village—'

The receiver was replaced.

Brenda went to work at the usual time. She had packed her suitcase in the night. She hadn't known what to do with Freda's things: her theatrical programmes and her jewel case with the plum stones. Her father said he would meet her at the station if she was sure what train she was arriving on.

'Need a spot of home comfort, do you?' he shouted down the phone in a jolly manner.

'Something like that,' Brenda had replied.

'Okey dokey, chickie,' he said. 'Mummy will be waiting.'

The lorry stood outside the bottle factory waiting for the loading to be finished. Maria was crying. Some men and a woman in a shabby coat lined the pavement.

'Stop crying,' said Vittorio, 'it is looking strange.'

Four men in green overalls, pushing a hogshead of sherry, appeared at the slant of the loading bay. Below in the street, a row of workers in mufflers and trilby hats stood waiting for the work to be finished.

'It's dreadful,' said Brenda. 'I think I shall faint.'

Mournful at the kerb, she put her hands to her face and watched the wooden barrel begin to roll down the slope. A dozen men with lowered heads lifted the hogshead on to the lorry. A plastic flower was laid on the lid. Papers were signed. Brenda, who was easily embarrassed, didn't want to be seen gawping in the road. She declined to look at the back of the lorry, grey with dust, as the last barrel was shoved into place.

'She's going,' cried Maria, and the engine started and the vehicle slid away from the bay, the plastic tulip lolling in the wind.